# Witch Is When All Was Revealed

D1527788

Published by Implode Publishing Ltd
© Implode Publishing Ltd 2016

# Chapter 1

When I arrived at Cuppy C, the twins had quite obviously been arguing *again*. They were standing at opposite ends of the counter—deliberately not looking at one another. I wasn't about to take sides, so I stood in the middle.

"Ahem. Any chance of service?"

"Amber can serve you." Pearl pointed at her sister. "I'm very busy."

"No you're not," Amber said. "You're not doing anything."

"You're not doing anything either."

"Girls, please! What's wrong now? Why have you fallen out, this time?"

"It's all Pearl's fault." Amber huffed.

"No it isn't. It's your fault. You've got no imagination."

"I've got plenty of imagination, thank you very much. You don't have any vision."

"I do so have vision."

"Please come here, both of you."

They shuffled slowly towards the centre of the counter until they were standing side by side. Neither of them would look at the other; instead, they stared straight ahead, at me.

"Which one of you is going to explain what's happened?"

"She can," Amber said.

"No, she can."

"Okay, this is what we're going to do." I didn't try to hide my exasperation. "We'll toss a coin. Call, Amber."

"Heads."

"Heads it is. Pearl, what's going on?"

"Are you sure that wasn't a double-headed coin?"

"Pearl!" I was about to lose it.

"Sorry, Jill. We've decided that Cuppy C needs a new name."

"What? You can't rename Cuppy C! It's a great name! Why would you want to change it?"

"It's a bit old and tired," Amber said, and then in a whisper, "A bit like Grandma."

"Yeah. We need something new and exciting," Pearl agreed.

"No, you don't. Look where *new and exciting* got you before. It got you the deluxe chocolate fountain that flooded this place, and a conveyor belt which managed to cover all your customers in cake."

"Yes, but that was different," Amber said. "We need a new brand; a new image."

"What name did you have in mind?"

"That's the problem." Pearl sighed. "Amber wants us to have a ridiculous name, while I've come up with a truly inspirational one."

"No, you haven't." Amber objected. "Your name is rubbish. My name is far better."

"Why don't we see which one Jill likes best?"

"Keep me out of this. I don't think you should change it at all."

"I think it should be Cake Calypso." Amber beamed. "Don't you think that's great?"

Before I could answer, Pearl jumped in. "I think it should be BunBun."

"BunBun?"

"Yeah, you know? Like the French sweet, bonbon, but

BunBun."

"It sounds like 'bumbum'." Amber giggled.

"No, it doesn't!" Pearl looked daggers at her sister.

"I see. So it's between Cake Calypso—"

"Which is brilliant, isn't it?" Amber interjected.

"Or BunBun."

"Which is much better," Pearl insisted. "Which one do you like best, Jill?"

"I don't like either of them. I like Cuppy C."

"We're not keeping Cuppy C. We're going to put it to the vote."

"And who exactly is going to vote?"

"The customers, of course. We're going to put up a poll on the notice board with both names on it, and ask them to pick the name they like the best. Whichever one has the most votes at the end of the week, will be the one we use."

"And that will be Cake Calypso," Amber said.

"No it won't. It'll be BunBun."

Oh dear. This had all the hallmarks of a disaster, but maybe there was still a way to avert it.

"Girls, I think the vote is a good idea, but I have a suggestion."

\*\*\*

"Mrs V? Whatever's the matter?" As soon as I walked into the office, I could tell that something was amiss.

"It's nothing, Jill".

"There's obviously something wrong. Is it your sister? Has she taken a turn for the worse?"

"No. G's fine. She's back home, and as good as new."

"What is it then? What's the problem?"

"It's Armi."

"What about him? He's not ill, is he?"

"No, he's okay."

"So, what is it?"

"It's just that—" She hesitated.

"Go on."

"It's that Gordon Armitage, again."

"I might have known. What's he done this time?"

"The other day when I went to Armi's office, Gordon must have seen me. Gordon told Armi that he didn't think it was a good idea for him to associate with anyone who worked with you."

"What a thoroughly horrible man Gordon Armitage is."

"You're right there."

"What does Armi have to say about all this?"

"He agrees that it's none of Gordon's business, but I get the feeling that he's a little intimidated."

"Why? Isn't Gordon his younger brother?"

"Yes, but you've seen the two of them. Gordon is an overbearing bully, and Armi is a meek, kind, quietly spoken man. He's no match for Gordon."

"How did you leave it?"

"Armi said that he'd give me a call, but I can't help but wonder if I'll ever hear from him again."

"You can't allow a bully like Gordon Armitage to come between you and Armi."

"It's out of my hands."

"Would you like me to have a word with Gordon?"

"No! Please, don't. I know that you feel you have to solve everyone's problems, but this is something that Armi and I have to resolve."

"But, I just—"

"No, Jill. Promise you'll keep out of it."

"But I could—"

"No! Let it go. We'll be okay. We've just got to ride this out."

"Okay, but keep me posted."

Despite the fact that she'd said I shouldn't get involved, I was sorely tempted to go next door, and give Gordon Armitage a piece of my mind. But that probably wasn't a good idea. If my track record was anything to go by, I'd only make things worse.

I was about to go through to my office when I spotted the newspaper on Mrs V's desk.

"How come you have a copy of The Bugle? Surely, you haven't started reading that awful rag?"

"I don't normally buy it, but they're running a yarn feature all this week—covering knitting and crocheting in Washbridge."

"Really? I wouldn't have thought that was The Bugle's kind of thing."

"Me neither. I was quite surprised when I saw it. Your grandmother has an article in here."

Wow! Grandma really did have Dougal Bugle wrapped around her little, bony finger.

"I say article, but it comes across as more of an advert for Ever A Wool Moment."

"That doesn't surprise me."

Just then, I noticed the front page headline: *'Where is Starr?'*

"Typical! They can't even spell Star," I tutted, but on closer inspection, I realised the article was actually about a reality TV celebrity called Starr Fish. She'd gone missing two days earlier, and no one knew her whereabouts. The article gave some background. Apparently, her real name was Carol Smith, but she'd changed it just before she took part in a reality TV show called 'Life At The Top', in which several young people were forced to live on the top floor of an apartment block. Essentially, they were stuck there together for six weeks while the cameras followed their exploits. Thankfully, I hadn't had the misfortune to see that terrible TV show, but apparently Starr Fish had won, and was now considered a Z-list celebrity. The speculation was that the pressure of 'fame' had got to her, and she was hiding from the glare of the spotlight.

The reason The Bugle was covering the story, which was probably more suited to the national tabloids, was because Starr lived in Washbridge. It seemed that Kathy wasn't the city's only reality TV celebrity.

Half way through the morning, Jack turned up at my office.

"What a nice surprise. Do you want a coffee?"

"I can't stay. I was just passing, and wanted to say that I'm looking forward to tonight's murder mystery evening."

"Huh?"

"Kathy called me earlier. She seemed to think I already knew about it."

"She did?"

"I said you must have forgotten to mention it."

"Yeah, I must have." Kathy was going to die a slow, lingering death.

"It'll be nice to pit my wits against yours. Anyway, like I said, I'm on my way somewhere. See you tonight, pet—"

"Don't you dare."

"Later." He grinned.

I waited until I heard him leave the outer office, and then called my sister.

"What's going on, Kathy?"

"Morning to you too, Jill. Yes, I'm very well — thanks for asking."

"Never mind that. What's all this about a murder mystery evening?"

"I thought I'd told you."

"Well, you didn't!

"Whoops! Silly me. It's being held at The Old Trout in Middle Tweaking."

"Middle whating?"

"Tweaking."

"What's that when it's at home?"

"It's the name of a village. It's about thirty miles from here. I'm surprised you haven't heard of it."

"I'm pretty sure I'd have remembered that name."

"I thought it sounded like fun. What with you being a P.I, and Jack being a detective."

"That's what we do for a living. It doesn't mean we want to spend our leisure time investigating murders. It's like asking Peter to go to a gardener's question time evening."

"Pete would probably enjoy that."

"So, what happens exactly?"

"First, we have a meal — the food is apparently excellent at The Old Trout. Then some local thesps entertain us. One of them pretends to have been murdered. We get to ask the others questions to work out which one of them is the murderer. Don't you think it sounds like fun?"

"I suppose so, but it would have been nice to have been

asked. And don't say you forgot because I don't believe you."

"It's about time the four of us had a night out together. How else are we ever going to get to know your future husband?"

"Goodbye, Kathy."

"Jill, wait! Have you seen the main story in The Bugle?"

"About Starr what's-her-face who's disappeared? What about it?"

"I can empathise with what she's going through."

I laughed. "Are you seriously trying to compare yourself to Starr Fish?"

"We're both reality TV celebrities."

"Yeah, but she's on the front page of all the national tabloids. You're on the back page of Crochet Monthly."

"I might have known you'd be jealous. Anyway, I *do* understand what it's like. All the fans—all the adoration. The pressure must've got to her. She's probably gone somewhere quiet to recuperate."

"All the fans? Are you kidding me? So far, you've had two old ladies ask you for an autograph."

"You're not counting all the autograph hunters who come into Ever A Wool Moment."

"How many have there been?"

"Loads."

"More than ten?"

"Probably."

\*\*\*

Mid-afternoon, I took myself out of the office for a while. There was something on my mind which I needed to think about without a crazy cat interrupting my thoughts.

I'd been shaken by what I'd seen on the top floor of The Central. If I'd understood the wall-calendar correctly, someone planned to take me out, in only a few days' time. My father had warned me that TDO was likely to act soon, but that could have been a double bluff to steer my attention away from him. I still couldn't shake the idea that *he* was TDO.

I found a quiet bench in Washbridge Gardens. I'd only been there for a few minutes when a little bird landed at my feet, and seemed to be waiting for me to feed him.

"Sorry, boy. I don't have any food."

It was as though he'd understood because he immediately flew away.

I needed help, but had no idea who to turn to. Normally, I would have gone to Grandma, but what could she do against TDO? The more I thought about it, the more I realised that I was on my own this time. I was going to have to face this threat alone, and hope that my new enhanced powers would be enough to see me through. It wasn't only my personal well-being that I feared for. I felt as though the future of Candlefield, and maybe even witchcraft itself, was on my shoulders. If I did succumb to TDO, and he absorbed my powers, who would be able to stand in his way?

\*\*\*

When I got back to my office, the room was in darkness. I tried the light switch, but nothing happened. What was going on? Then, I heard the sound of someone striking a match. Winky lit the two candles which were standing on a table in the middle of the office. Now, I could see why it was so dark. Blackout curtains had been hung over the window, and someone had removed the light bulbs.

"Ahem! Excuse me."

"I thought you'd gone home," he said.

"Why would I have gone home already?"

"Because you don't have any cases to work on?"

"Never mind that. Why is there a table and chairs in the middle of my office?"

"It was a bit too draughty near the window."

"I don't mean why are they in the centre of the room. I mean, why are they here at all?"

"I'm making preparations for dinner this evening."

"Dinner? Who for?"

"Myself and Katrina."

"Who's Katrina?"

"I thought I'd already told you. She's my potential new girlfriend."

"You never mentioned any Katrina to me."

"It must have slipped my mind."

There seemed to be a lot of *mind slipping* going on around me.

"Where did you find Katrina?"

"On Purrfect Match."

"Have you met her already?"

"No. We've exchanged e-mails, and we've chatted online, but she said that she didn't want to use Skype. She said she'd rather we saw each other for the first time 'in the fur,' so to speak." He laughed at his own joke—no one else was going to.

"So what time is Katrina coming over?"

"Six o'clock."

"Don't you think you should have asked my permission before you arranged this?"

"You would probably have said no."

"That's the whole point of asking permission. What about the catering? You're not going to be cooking in here, are you?" I glanced around in case he'd hidden an oven somewhere.

"Don't worry. I've placed an order with Feline Supreme Cuisine."

"That sounds very expensive."

"It is, but first impressions and all that."

"Please tell me you didn't use my credit card to pay for the meal?"

"Of course I didn't."

Phew! "Thank goodness for that."

"They charge extra for credit card payments, so I used your debit card instead. See how considerate I am?"

"How much is tonight's dinner costing me?"

"It was very reasonable."

"How much, Winky?"

"Considering all the ingredients are sourced locally."

"Winky, how much?"

"Not more than thirty pounds."

"Thirty pounds?"

"Each."

"You're going to bankrupt me, and where will you live then?"

"You're always so melodramatic."

"Okay. I know you're still upset about Bella, so I'm going to turn a blind eye to this one." I laughed. "Get it? Blind eye?" I closed one of my eyes.

"Are you mocking me?"

"As if I'd be so insensitive. Look, this has to be a one-off. Agreed?"

"Anything you say."

"In that case, I hope your evening with Katrina goes well."

"Don't worry. Casanova Winky has still got it."

# Chapter 2

Middle Tweaking? I hated those stupid, twee, village names. I'd wanted to take my car or Jack's, and to meet Kathy and Peter there, but she wasn't having any of it. She'd insisted we all go together. Peter was driving, which meant that she'd try to interrogate Jack all the way there. Not if I had anything to do with it. I'd warned Jack what to expect.

"If she starts asking you lots of questions, tell her to mind her own business."

"How am I supposed to do that, Jill? She's your sister; I barely know her. What kind of first impression will it be if I tell her to mind her own business every time she asks a question?"

"You have to be blunt with Kathy. She doesn't take hints."

"I'm sure she isn't nearly as bad as you're painting her."

She was, but to my surprise and delight, Peter came to our rescue. Although he was driving, he must have known what Kathy had in store for us, so he carried the conversation all the way there. Kathy was getting angrier and angrier because she was desperate to get in some personal questions. As Jack and I walked across the car park, I could hear her giving Peter a real ear bashing.

Situated between the post office and the butcher, The Old Trout was pretty much what you'd expect of a small village pub. That kind of local pub can often be quite unwelcoming—full of locals who aren't fond of outsiders. But The Old Trout wasn't at all like that; there was a healthy mix of locals and tourists. The pub was aptly named; all of the walls were covered in fishing memorabilia and photographs, all of the same man. In most of them he was holding either a large fish or a trophy.

Moments later, that very man appeared behind the bar.

"Welcome to The Old Trout. My name's Trevor Total."

Trevor Total? T. Total? I loved it! Maybe I was going to enjoy this night more than I'd expected.

"Are you fine ladies and gentlemen here for the murder mystery evening?"

"We are," Peter said.

"In that case, you need to go through to the function room in the back. Through that door." He pointed. "Someone will be around shortly to take your drink and food orders. The murder mystery should get underway within the next thirty minutes or so."

Just like in the main room, the function room walls were covered in all kinds of fishing memorabilia: rods, keep nets, floats, flies and dozens of framed photographs of our host.

"Did you notice what his name was?" I said, when we'd taken our seats.

"Trevor Total, wasn't it?" Kathy said.

"Yeah. Don't you get it? Trevor Total. T. Total."

The three of them stared at me—nonplussed.

"Teetotal, as in, doesn't drink. Mr T Total—never mind." What was wrong with these people?

There was a set menu. I went for the chicken. Jack chose the steak, so did Peter. Kathy went for the lamb. The format of the evening was that the 'players' would introduce themselves before the meal. Then, after we'd eaten, the players would return to the small stage at the far end of the function room, and we'd all get an opportunity to try to discover who the murderer was.

"Well, Jack," Kathy said. "I'm glad we've actually got to meet you properly at last."

Oh dear, here we go. Peter might have held her off during the car journey, but there would be no stopping her now.

"It's nice to meet you two, too. Jill has told me a lot about you both."

"All bad, no doubt."

"Most of it," I chimed in.

"We've heard a lot about you too, Jack." Kathy was on a roll. "In the early days, my sister thought you were evil incarnate. What was it you used to call him, Jill?"

I shot her a look. "I'm sure I didn't call him anything."

"It's okay." Jack laughed. "It can't have been any worse than some of the things I used to call Jill. I'd never met such a royal pain in the bum."

"Gee thanks."

"That's all behind us now," he said. "We seem to have reached an understanding."

"Is *that* what you call it?" Kathy gave him a knowing look.

Much to my relief, the MC, Trevor Total, took to the stage.

"Ladies and gentlemen, before you enjoy your meals, I'd like to take this opportunity to introduce you to tonight's players who will be performing the last ever murder mystery to be held at The Old Trout. Please welcome them on stage. Firstly, we have Mr Brendan Breeze, the fishmonger here in Middle Tweaking."

There was a polite round of applause as Brendan joined

the MC on stage.

"Next, we have Mr Harry Payne, the local butcher. And our postmistress, Madge Hick."

I laughed, and Kathy glared at me. "Didn't you hear her name? Madge Hick? Get it? Magic?"

"You're such a child sometimes," Kathy said, under her breath.

"Next, we have Florence Long who runs the pharmacy. And finally, Justin Flower, the baker."

Just in flour? This night was getting better and better.

All of the players looked thoroughly miserable—as though they didn't want to be there.

"Thank you, ladies and gentlemen. We'll leave you now to enjoy your food. Afterwards, we'll begin the murder mystery."

"Madge Hick is the murderer," I said.

"How can you know that?" Kathy asked. "They haven't done anything yet."

"I have a nose for this sort of thing. You forget that I'm a professional. I can pick out a murderer from a mile away."

"But it's not a real murder. You can't apply the same rules here."

"We'll see. Just mark my words. Madge Hick is the murderer."

They all looked doubtful—even Jack. They'd soon see I was right.

The food was delicious. The only thing spoiling it was that Kathy continued with her interrogation.

"Tell me, Jack. Have you met any of Jill's birth family?"

"No, I haven't. Jill doesn't really talk about them. I did hear about her cousins the other day, though. They run a cake shop, apparently."

"You mean Diamond and Emerald?" Kathy said.

"It's Amber and Pearl." I corrected her.

"Is it any wonder I've forgotten their names? I met them once, but that was ages ago." She turned back to Jack. "Jill never talks about her birth family, and I know for a fact she has an aunt and a grandmother. I had hoped that me, Pete and the kids might get to visit them, but every time I mention it, Jill changes the subject."

"I do not change the subject! Who do you think will win the Oscars this year?"

"There you go again! Wouldn't you like to meet her birth family, Jack?"

"Definitely."

This conversation was headed in a bad direction. If I didn't put a stop to it quickly, it could spiral out of control. I did the only thing I could under the circumstances; I cast a powerful 'forget' spell on all three of them.

"What was I saying?" Kathy looked understandably puzzled.

"You were telling Jack about Lizzie's talent competition," I prompted.

"Was I? Oh yes. Lizzie entered a talent competition the other week and did really well. And she's just entered another one. You should get Jill to bring you along."

"Jack's too busy." I couldn't subject him to that.

"Not necessarily," Jack said. "If I can get away, I'd love to hear her sing."

That's what you think.

"She has a beautiful voice," Kathy said.

Once everyone had finished their meals, and the tables

had been cleared, the MC returned to the stage. "Ladies and gentlemen, it's time for you to solve tonight's murder mystery."

With that, the lights in the function room went down. I could barely see my hand in front of me. Then, from somewhere, came a short burst of dramatic music. Moments later, when the lights came back on, there was someone lying on the stage. Behind her, stood the other players.

"Oh look, Jill." Kathy grinned. "It looks like your murderer is actually the victim."

She was right. Madge Hick was lying prone on the stage.

"So much for your brilliant powers of deduction."

All three of them had a laugh at my expense. I glared at Jack — the traitor!

"Right, ladies and gentlemen." The MC took centre-stage again. "Now, each of you in turn will be allowed to ask questions of any of the players. You're allowed to ask them anything related to their relationship with the victim, or about their movements over the last few hours. So, I'll throw it open to the room. Who would like to ask the first question?"

I immediately put my hand up.

"Yes, young lady?" The MC pointed to me. "Which of our players would you like to ask a question?"

"Her!" I pointed to the woman lying on the floor.

"You can't ask the victim a question."

Kathy elbowed me in the side. "Jill, you're showing us up."

"I'm not convinced she's dead. I think it's a trick."

The MC looked put out. "This *is* the victim, and she is

most certainly dead. You'll have to pick one of the other players."

"Okay then. I'll ask the fishmonger a question."

Brendan Breeze took a step forward. "Ask away."

"Was the victim a customer of yours?"

"Yes, Madge often came into my shop. She loved her fish."

"What was her favourite fish?"

"She was particularly partial to red herring."

Everybody laughed.

"When did you last see her?"

"Yesterday. She came into the shop, and bought some eels."

I was about to ask another question when the MC interrupted me.

"Sorry young lady, but you can't commandeer the whole evening."

Over the next hour, everyone fired questions at the players. Supposedly their answers would give clues to the murderer. The problem was that most of the questions asked were useless. Questions like: 'what's your favourite colour?' and 'what's your favourite TV program?'

What use was that? No self-respecting investigator would ask a question like that. Even Jack asked trivial questions; I was very disappointed in him.

When the MC called time on the questioning, we had to vote for who we thought the murderer was by writing the name on a slip of paper. I still thought Madge Hick was the murderer, but I wasn't allowed to vote for her, so I went for Justin Flower. There was something about him that smacked of murderer. Kathy went for Brendan Breeze. So did Peter, but only because Kathy told him to.

Jack went for Harry Payne which was a stupid choice. It obviously wasn't the butcher.

"Ladies and gentlemen. We have collected together the votes, and I can tell you that only one person has correctly picked out the murderer."

No surprises there. After all, I was the only professional in the room — no offence, Jack.

The players, other than Madge Hick, moved to the back of the stage.

"And the murderer is — " The MC paused for dramatic effect. "Harry Payne!"

Payne took a bow. Everyone clapped — except me.

"The only person who correctly picked the murderer tonight was Mr Jack Maxwell. Jack, where are you?"

"Stand up, Jack." Kathy nudged him.

He stood up, and looked a little embarrassed.

"Well done, sir." The MC led the applause. "You win a bottle of champagne."

"Jill, why aren't you clapping?" Kathy glared at me.

"Sorry." I clapped rather half-heartedly.

"Well done, Jack," Peter said.

"Yeah, well done, Jack." Kathy nodded.

She and Peter both looked at me.

"Yeah, well done." I suppose.

"Well," Jack said, "I guess that only goes to show. You should leave these things to the professionals." Then he winked at me.

The whole thing was obviously totally bogus.

# Chapter 3

Looking back on it the next morning, the murder mystery evening hadn't been quite the disaster I'd expected it to be, even though I'd had to endure a certain amount of mocking because I'd failed to pick out the murderer. Or at least, the person they claimed to be the murderer. I still had my doubts.

The most difficult part of the evening had been the questions about my birth family. The 'forget' spell had got me out of that jam, but it was an ongoing problem, and one I was going to have to address if Jack and I were ever to have any kind of meaningful, long-term relationship. I could always get the twins and Aunt Lucy to come over to Washbridge to meet him. And, Grandma spent almost as much time in the human world as I did. But, eventually he was bound to ask why we never went to visit them. Being in a long-term relationship with a human wasn't going to be easy. Maybe, I should talk to the girls at Love Spell. They presumably encountered this same problem all the time with the witches they matched up with humans.

My head was spinning just thinking about it. That's probably why I didn't sleep very well; I was tossing and turning all night. In my dream, Jack was trying to follow me to Candlefield.

I was eating breakfast—only half awake, when Kathy phoned. She was no doubt going to rub it in about my failure in the murder mystery.

"Jill, have you seen the news?"

"Not yet. What's happened?"

"Apparently, Madge Hick has been murdered in Middle Tweaking."

"Very funny. You're hilarious. Did you really ring me at this time of day just to have another laugh at my expense?"

"I'm not kidding. She really has been murdered."

"How do you mean, murdered?"

"It's not a difficult concept to grasp. She's dead. Someone killed her."

"For real?"

"Yes, for real. Check the local news. They found her body in the early hours of this morning. Anyway, I've got to see to the kids. I just thought I should let you know."

The main story on the local TV news was indeed the murder in Middle Tweaking. Madge Hick, the postmistress, had been found dead in her flat above the post office in the early hours of the morning. I gave Jack a call to see what he made of it.

"Have you heard about the murder in Middle Tweaking?"

"Yes. We received word a short time ago."

"Are you going to be working the case?"

"No, it's outside our area. We won't be involved."

"Don't you think it's a bit creepy that last night Madge Hick was the victim in a murder mystery, and now she's been murdered for real?"

"A little, yes, but when you've been in the job as long as I have, nothing surprises you anymore."

"I guess."

"I had a really good time last night, Jill. I really like Kathy and Peter. Kathy's a hoot!"

"She is when she's not trying to interrogate you."

"You're too hard on her. She's your sister. Of course she's interested in what you do."

"She's not *interested*. She's *nosy*."

"And you're not?"

"When am I ever nosy?"

"Obviously never." He laughed. "Okay, well I've got to get to work even if *you* haven't. I'll catch up with you later."

***

"Mrs V, you've had your hair done."

"Do you like it?"

"It's very — blue."

"But do you think it suits me?"

Blue hair had never suited anyone — not even the Smurfs. "Yes, it looks — err — great."

"I thought it was time for a change."

"Would that have anything to do with a certain gentleman in an office not too far from here?"

"It might have."

"Have you heard from Armi, then?"

"He gave me a call late last night to say he was sorry he hadn't been around. He'd thought it best to let the dust settle for a while."

"Good for Armi. I'm glad to hear that he's not letting that despicable brother of his bully him. I'm sure he'll love your hair." Always providing he's colour blind.

When I opened the door to my office, I heard the sound of balls dropping to the floor.

"Great! Thanks very much, Jill." Winky glared at me.

"What have I done now?"

"I was juggling."

"Of course you were. How remiss of me not to knock

first—just in case you were juggling."

"I'm practising for a world record attempt, and now I'm going to have to start all over again."

"I'm very sorry about that, but this *is* my office."

"Couldn't you have just waited for another five minutes?"

"You should have put a notice on the door: *'Cat juggling – do not disturb'*."

"Now you're just being silly."

"Anyway, how did your date with Katrina go?"

"Not great."

"Didn't you hit it off?"

"She slurps her milk."

"That's not good."

"Tell me about it. And she burps."

"Gross!"

"I know. I couldn't possibly live with that. I mean, she's very pretty, but I couldn't focus with all the slurping and burping."

"So you won't be seeing her again, I take it?"

"I said I'd call her."

"That's rather a cowardly way out. Why didn't you just tell her you don't want to see her again?"

"Oh yeah. And what would I have said when she asked why? *It's because you slurp your milk, and burp?'* I'm not sure that would have gone down very well."

"I guess you're right. Where does that leave you, date-wise?"

"I've got a few other candidates on my Purrfect Match list, so I'm hoping to arrange another date soon. What about you? How did your foursome go?"

"I'd rather you didn't refer to it as a foursome."

"How many of you were there?"

"Four, but—"

"That's a foursome in my book. So, was it a roaring success?"

"It wasn't as bad as I expected."

"That good, eh?"

"It would've been okay if Kathy hadn't kept bringing up the subject of my birth family, and asking why she never got to visit them."

"Oh yeah, I'd forgotten about that. You have to hide your witch stuff from your sister, don't you?"

"And from Jack now, too. It's not easy."

"What about the murder mystery? Did you pick out the murderer?"

"Of course. I was the only one who did."

What? Of course I wasn't lying. I was just being economical with the truth.

* * *

I had zero cases to work on, so halfway through the morning, I decided to take a trip over to Candlefield—a blueberry muffin was called for.

Amber and Pearl were sitting at a window table. They looked very serious, and were deep in conversation. I hadn't intended to interrupt them, but they spotted me at the counter and called me over.

"Hi, girls. Is something wrong?"

"What gave it away?"

"Is there a problem with Cuppy C?"

"No, the shop's doing okay. We had the origami demonstration yesterday afternoon. We thought you might have dropped by to watch it."

"I really wanted to." Like I wanted a hole in the head. "But I've been so busy; you know how it is. How did it go?"

"It was better than the pottery day."

"That's good. Did many people turn up?"

"More than for the pottery day."

"Right. So, how many people altogether?"

"Including us?"

"Yes."

"And, including the two assistants we brought in specially to deal with the crowds?"

"Yes."

"Eleven."

"So, that's you two, plus the two assistants. Eleven minus four. That's seven?"

"More or less."

"Less actually." Amber sighed. "Two of them were here to clean the windows."

"I'm not sure these craft days are working out, girls."

"We've come to the same conclusion. They can't compete with Miles Best's circus performers. We need to have a re-think."

"Is he still running the circus days, then?"

"Yes, and they seem to be doing really well. Some of our regular customers were talking about it the other day. They said how much they enjoyed the fire eaters."

"Is that why you two are so down in the dumps?"

"No, it's got nothing to do with the shop."

"What then?"

"It's Alan," Pearl said.

"And William," Amber said.

"What's the matter? Are they both okay?"

"Yes." Amber sighed. "Except that they're not talking to us."

"Neither of them? Why?"

"You remember how we told you about the double wedding?"

"Yes."

"Apparently, we should have told them, too."

Oh dear.

"We kind of forgot," Pearl said.

"They are rather integral to the event. Don't you think it would have been nice to let them know that you were planning a double wedding?"

"With hindsight, yes, we probably should have." Pearl conceded. "But we were too busy thinking about the important things, like what colour dresses to wear, and what flowers we wanted, and what food to order for the reception."

"But, not your future husbands?"

"You're really not helping, Jill. You make it sound like we were in the wrong."

"You kind of were. What's happening with them, now?"

"They're not sure if they want a double wedding or not. They want time to think about it."

"So, it might be off?"

"Not if we have anything to do with it. We just have to talk them around. We can usually wrap them around our little fingers; we'll come up with something."

"I just bet you will. By the way, how did the vote go for the new name?"

"We've changed our minds about that," Amber said.

"Really? You both seemed so keen."

"Nah. We're not going to bother." Pearl shrugged.

"Wait a minute." I could smell something, and it seemed awfully rat-like. "What happened with the vote?"

The twins looked at one another.

"I'm not going to let up until you tell me."

"It's all your fault, anyway," Amber blurted out.

"My fault? What did *I* do?"

"You were the one who said we should include the third option," Pearl said.

"Yeah, we just wanted to have them vote on the two names," Amber agreed.

"So you did include the third option—to keep the name?"

"Yeah." They both nodded.

"So how many votes did 'Cuppy C' get?"

"I don't remember," Amber said.

"Okay. I'll make it easy for you. How many votes did the other two names get?"

"They both received the same number of votes," Amber said.

"Yeah." Pearl nodded. "People liked both of our names equally."

"How many people?"

"I don't remember exactly."

"Was it more than twenty?"

They shook their heads.

"More than ten?"

They shook their heads again.

"Was it more than—"

"Okay, okay, if you must know," Pearl interrupted. "It was two."

"Two?" I laughed. "That wasn't you two, by any chance, was it?"

They glared at me.

"Priceless! How many voted for Cuppy C?"

"One hundred and seventy-six."

"So, a close-run thing, then?"

"No one likes a smarty-pants," Amber said, under her breath.

"I still think BunBun is better," Pearl said.

Just then, Daze rang me.

"Where are you, Jill?"

"I'm in Calypso BunBun."

The twins looked daggers at me.

"Huh?"

"Sorry, I meant Cuppy C."

"Good. I'm only a couple of minutes away. Can I come and talk to you?"

"Yes, of course. Come on over."

When Daze arrived, she grabbed a coffee, and we took a table on the opposite side of the shop from the twins, who were still debating how best to talk their fiancés around.

"I wanted to bring you up to speed about your father," Daze said. "And to let you know that I won't be able to follow him anymore. I'm stacked with other work."

"That's okay. I appreciate what you've done so far. Is there anything else to report?"

"No, not really. I followed him yesterday and again today, but he hasn't been anywhere in particular or met with anyone. He walked the same circular route around Candlefield, and went past The Central, but he didn't disappear this time."

"Right, thanks again, Daze."

I wondered if I should tell her that I'd actually managed to get inside The Central, and what I'd seen in there. In the end, I decided against it; this was something I had to handle alone.

*** 

Winky was busy trying to set a personal best for his juggling. He gave me the evil eye every time he dropped one of the balls as though somehow it was my fault. As there was still nothing happening work-wise, I decided to call it a day early.

I planned to call in at the newsagent to pick up a bottle of ginger beer, but before I could get across the road, I bumped into Betty Longbottom and Luther Stone who were arm in arm. I still couldn't get my head around the idea that they were now a couple.

"Hello, Jill." Betty was so smug since she'd taken up with Luther. Not that I was bitter. At all.

"Hello there, you two."

"Hi, Jill," Luther said. "Where are you off to?"

"Just to the newsagent. I'm having a quiet night in. Just me, a bottle of ginger beer, and a few custard creams."

"Guess where we're going," Betty said.

"To an accountants' convention?"

"Nothing as boring as that." Luther grinned. "Betty's taking me to my first ever seashell exhibition."

"And, you're going of your own free will?"

"Of course. Until I met Betty, I never realised there was such a variety of shapes and colours. It really is fascinating. I'm hoping to make a few purchases while we're there—to kick-start my own collection. Luckily, I've got Betty to advise me; she's something of an expert when it comes to sea shells."

"That is lucky."

How had sexy, red-hot Luther turned into boring seashell man? Perhaps Betty was some kind of sup. Maybe she'd cast a 'boring' spell on him? Or maybe he'd caught it from Mr Ivers? Was *boring* contagious?

After a couple more minutes of riveting sea-shell conversation, I'd lost the will to live, so I made my excuses, and went over to the newsagent where as usual Jasper James was behind the counter. Today's fedora was lime green.

"I have to ask, Jasper, how many fedoras do you own?"

"That's a sore point. Mrs James says I have too many. She insists that using the spare room just for my fedoras is not a good use of space."

"It sounds like you have an awful lot of them."

"A lifetime's collection, but I'm always on the lookout for new ones. If you spot any on your travels, I hope you'll tip me off. I'm particularly interested in locating a gold one. They're exceedingly rare."

"I'll keep my eyes open for you."

"What can I get for you today?"

"Just a bottle of ginger beer, please."

"Surely you're not going to leave without a magazine?"

"I'm not really in the mood for reading today."

"Are you sure? Couldn't I interest you in this one? It seems to be extremely popular at the moment." He lifted it from the shelf. "Seashell Weekly. I've had a second subscription for this only today."

"Could that have been Mr Luther Stone, by any chance?"

"It was indeed. He already subscribes to Accountant

Talk and Accountant Bi-weekly, but now he seems to have developed a new interest. It must be that new girlfriend of his. She subscribes to a number of sea creature-related magazines: Jellyfish Digest, Crustaceans Quarterly, and a couple of others. Are you sure you're not interested?"

"I'll just take the ginger beer, thanks."

# Chapter 4

Mrs V popped her head around the door. Maybe the blue look would grow on me eventually? A bit like fungus.

"There's a lady here to see you, Jill. A Ms Turtle."

"Oh? Okay. Send her in." I wasn't expecting anyone, but hopefully this could be a new case.

Ms Turtle was dressed in a tweed two-piece. I put her in her late sixties, maybe even early seventies. Her serious expression gave nothing away.

"Jill Gooder, I assume?"

"That's right."

"The sign outside says 'Ken Gooder'?"

"Ken was my father. This used to be his business; he died some time ago, but I haven't got around to changing the sign yet."

"Hmm? Not very efficient."

This wasn't getting off to a very good start.

"Please take a seat, Ms Turtle."

"Thank you."

"Would you like tea, or coffee?"

"Tea would be very nice."

"Milk and sugar?"

"Milk and one and three quarters spoonfuls of sugar."

A kindred spirit! I was beginning to warm to this old lady.

"I'll ask Mrs V to make us some."

"Mrs V?"

"My receptionist."

"Is there something wrong with her hair? It seems to have turned blue."

"I don't think so. Excuse me for just a minute."

"Mrs V. Can I have two teas, please. Milk in both. One and two thirds spoonfuls of sugar for me." She rolled her eyes as she always did. "And one and three quarters spoonfuls for Ms Turtle. See—" I grinned. "It isn't just me."

I left Mrs V tutting about sugar measures, and re-joined Ms Turtle.

"Is that your cat?"

She'd spotted Winky, who had just crawled out from under the leather sofa.

"Yeah, that's Winky."

"What a handsome young man he is. Come here, boy."

She put out her hand, and Winky came strolling over. While Ms Turtle made a fuss of him, and in between purrs, he turned to me and said, "I like this old bird."

"Shush."

"What?" Ms Turtle looked a little affronted.

"Sorry, I was just sneezing."

"What a very strange sneeze you have."

"It's sort of a family thing. What is it I can do for you, Ms Turtle?"

"I came here on the bus from Middle Tweaking."

She probably wanted to hire me to investigate the murder of Madge Hick. News of my reputation had obviously spread further afield than I thought.

"I see. I assume you're here about the murder of Madge Hick?"

"I am indeed." She handed me a business card from her handbag. On it was printed: 'Myrtle Turtle', and her phone number.

"Myrtle?"

"Yes?"

"Turtle."

"Yes."

"Nice name." I stifled a laugh. "May I call you Myrtle?"

"All my friends call me Myrtle."

"Right."

"You can call me Ms Turtle."

"Oh? Right. I assume you'd like to hire me to investigate Madge Hick's murder?"

"Hire you? No. Why would I hire *you*?"

Huh?

"Because I'm a private investigator? Isn't that why you came to see me?"

"No. I'm here to ask you some questions. *I'm* investigating the murder, and I was told by some of the people who were in The Old Trout that you were a little unconventional in your approach."

"What do you mean *unconventional*?"

"Didn't you accuse the victim of being the murderer?"

"Oh that? I suppose so, but—"

"Don't you think that's rather unconventional? Did you think the victim had murdered herself?"

"No, of course not. I thought it was some kind of double bluff."

"Is that how you approach your real life cases?"

"Well, no. I—err—"

"Did you know Madge Hick?"

"No. I'd never seen her before that night."

"Are you sure?"

Sheesh. What was with the third degree? "I'm sure."

"Had you been to Middle Tweaking before?"

"No. I'd never even heard of the place."

"What did you do after the murder mystery evening had finished?"

"We came straight back to Washbridge. Peter, my brother-in-law, drove. He dropped me off at my flat."

"I see. And after that?"

"I went to bed. It was the next morning when I heard that Madge Hick had been murdered."

She scribbled something in a notebook, and looked at me — rather suspiciously I thought.

Mrs V brought in the tea. "This one has one and three-quarters — wait, no — two-thirds — or maybe this one. I'll just put the tray down here. You can sort them out, Jill." With that, she scurried away.

I took a sip out of the cup closest to me; Ms Turtle took a sip from the one nearest to her.

"I think we've got each other's, dear." She screwed up her face.

"You're right, Ms Turtle."

We swapped cups.

"Much better," she said. "One and three quarters just hits the mark."

"Look, I'm not sure how to say this, Ms Turtle, but investigating a murder can be very demanding. Even I find it hard going sometimes, and I'm young. For someone such as yourself — "

"Hold it right there, young lady. Are you trying to suggest that I'm not up to running a murder investigation? I've probably solved more murders than you've had men friends."

That wouldn't be difficult.

"Is this something you do as a hobby?" I asked.

"I would hardly call it a hobby, more a vocation."

"I see."

"So why were you at the murder mystery evening, Miss Gooder?"

There was something distinctly weird about being interrogated in my own office.

"Please call me Jill."

"The question remains."

"It was actually my sister's idea. I wasn't too keen to be honest."

"Will she vouch for that?"

"Yes, of course."

The old girl grilled me for another thirty minutes. I felt like she'd put me through the wringer.

"Right, well thank you for your time, Miss Gooder. I'd better get going. The buses to Middle Tweaking don't run very often."

"Maybe I could be of some assistance?"

"I'm quite capable of catching a bus, young lady."

"I didn't mean with the bus. It's very unusual, but I don't have much work on at the moment." Winky laughed, but I ignored him. "So I have a little time on my hands. Maybe I could come over to Middle Tweaking to help with your investigation?"

"What makes you think I need any help?"

"I didn't mean that. I just meant—"

"If you're struggling for work, and you think you'd benefit from working alongside me, then you're welcome to come over and watch an expert at work."

The poor old girl had delusions of grandeur. How many murders could she really have solved? None, was my guess. But this could prove to be an interesting case, and it might generate a few positive headlines in the press, which was always good for business. Even though I wouldn't be paid, it was better than sitting around the office, twiddling my thumbs. I'd humour her, and pretend I was going to let her give me the benefit of her experience. Then, after I'd solved the murder, I'd be sure to give her a little credit. I'm generous like that.

"Okay, Ms Turtle. I'd like that."

"I live in the old watermill. Everyone knows it; just ask anyone in the village."

She finished her tea, bid me farewell, and went to catch her bus.

"A new client?" Mrs V enquired, after Ms Turtle had left.

"Not exactly. She's a little delusional. She thinks she's some kind of sleuth."

"A bit like you, then?"

It was at times like these that I remembered why I didn't pay Mrs V.

***

I'd popped out of the office for a while to clear my head, and to stock up on custard creams, when I bumped into Bonnie and Clive.

"Hello, you two."

They looked remarkably happy under the circumstances. I thought they'd still be in mourning for the loss of their feline catwalk superstar, Bella. Far from it; they were all smiles, and looked pleased to see me.

"Hello, Jill," Clive said. "We really should have come over to tell you our good news."

"Good news?"

"Bella is back with us."

"Really?"

"She came back a couple of days ago. I opened the front door to get the newspaper, and there she was. It's as though she's never been away. We're so happy, aren't we, Bonnie?"

Bonnie certainly looked much happier than the last time I'd seen her.

"That's really good news. I'm so pleased for you both."

"You must let us buy you a little present, as a thank you."

"Really, no. I wouldn't hear of it." How little? Not too little, I hoped.

"We'll drop something off at your office, later."

"Only if you insist."

I had to get back to the office to tell Winky the good news; he'd be so thrilled.

I rushed up the stairs, and whizzed past Mrs V, who looked at me as though I'd lost my mind. Again.

"Winky! You'll never guess what?"

"You've got a paying case?"

"No, much more exciting than that. Bella's back!"

"Oh, that." He shrugged. "I already knew."

"You did? How long have you known?"

"Since yesterday."

"And, you didn't think to tell me?"

"Why would I tell you?"

"Because I was the mug who spent hours creating posters, and putting them up all over Washbridge to try to get her back. I was the one who sympathised with you when your brother ran away with her. Didn't you think I deserved to know?"

He shrugged again.

"So what happened?" I asked.

"The usual story. Socks got bored with her; like he does with all of his ladies. He dumped her. Poor old Bella had to make her way back to Washbridge."

"But she's okay?"

"As far as I know."

"Have you spoken to her?"

"Briefly, she gave me a call."

"Are you two back together again?"

"It's not as easy as that. The cut runs very deep. Have you forgotten she ran off with my brother? I've told her that I'll need a little time to think it over."

Mrs V had asked if she could pop out for a few minutes. She wanted to pay a visit to Ever A Wool Moment to change some of the colours in her Everlasting Wool subscription. While she was gone, I sat at her desk for a while—for a change of scenery, and also because Winky was getting more and more tetchy at his inability to beat his personal best juggling record.

While in the outer office, I heard voices out on the landing. It was Gordon Armitage, and Armi.

"I've told you, Joseph, you should have nothing to do with that woman."

"But, Gordon, we're in love."

"Don't be ridiculous. You haven't known her long enough to be in love with her. And besides, she works for that dreadful private investigator. I want you to have nothing more to do with her."

"But, Gordon, Annabel and I—"

"I said you're to drop her! Do you hear me?"

"But, Gordon—"

"I don't want to hear any more about it, and I do not expect you to see her again."

Poor old Armi. He stood no chance against that bully, Gordon. It made me so angry. I couldn't let Gordon Armitage spoil what Mrs V and Armi had going; I had to do something about it. Mrs V had warned me off, and made me promise to stay out of it, but how could I?

When I opened the door, Gordon had gone, but Armi was still standing there. He looked shell shocked after the tongue lashing he'd just received.

"Oh? Hello, Jill."

"Are you okay, Armi?"

"Not really. I'm afraid I may have to stop seeing Annabel."

"I'm sure that won't be necessary." I cast a spell. "Why don't you give it some thought before you rush into anything."

He looked a little dazed; the spell was obviously starting to take effect. "Okay. Maybe you're right. Thanks, Jill."

# Chapter 5

The twins and Aunt Lucy regularly took Barry for a walk, so I knew he was getting plenty of exercise, but he was meant to be my dog, and it seemed ages since I'd taken him out.

The twins were busy behind the counter in Cuppy C, so I didn't like to disturb them. I just went straight upstairs.

"Jill! Jill! Can we go for a walk?" Barry was all over me. "Jill! I want to go to the park. Can we see Babs? Can we go for a walk now, please?"

You always knew where you stood with Barry; he never changed. Crazy as a box of crazy frogs.

"Yes, we'll go to the park now."

"Can we see Babs?"

"Sorry, no. It'll be just you and me, today. I think Babs is still away with Dolly."

"Aww! I want to see Babs!"

"Do you want to go to the park or not?"

"Yes! Let's go to the park. I want to go for a walk. Let's go for a walk."

Barry dragged me every step of the way as per usual. When we reached the park, I let him off the lead, and off he ran. I sat on a bench; I knew that in time, he'd wear himself out and come find me.

I'd been there for no more than twenty minutes when I spotted a dog that I recognised. It was Babs. She was on the lead, but I didn't recognise the man who was walking her. Had he stolen her? I had to find out before he disappeared with her.

"Excuse me," I called. "Hello, there!"

The man was obviously wondering if he knew me.

"Hello?"

"My name's Jill Gooder. Is that Babs?"

"It is. Do you know her?"

"Yes. My dog, Barry, often goes for a walk with her."

"You must be the private investigator lady?"

"That's me."

"Dolly told me all about you. I believe you've helped Dorothy."

"That's right. And you are?"

"Sorry. I'm Nigel West. I—err—and Dolly—we—err—are kind of an item. We've been seeing each other for quite some time."

"I'm sorry. I didn't realise. Dorothy has never mentioned you."

"Unfortunately, Dorothy and I don't get on very well."

"I see."

"You know how it is. Children don't like to think of their parents having a love life. Dorothy was used to having Dolly all to herself. When I came onto the scene, it rather put her nose out of joint. To keep the peace, we've kept our relationship very low key. But now Dorothy's gone to live in the human world—well, that changes everything." He grinned.

"I see. Have you moved in?"

"No. It's a little early for that, but we certainly see a lot more of each other."

"Where is Dolly? Is she still at the artists' retreat?"

"No. She came back yesterday—much re-energised from the experience. When I left her just now, she was in her studio. She's got a commission today."

"A paid commission?"

"Yes. A vampire couple are having their portraits

done."

Oh dear.

"Anyway, I'd better get going," Nigel said. "I promised Dolly I'd be back in time to make drinks for everyone."

"Right. Well, it was nice to meet you, Nigel. Bye!"

I went back to the bench. A couple of minutes later, my phone rang.

"Is that Jill Gooder?" A squeaky little voice said.

"Squeaking, I mean speaking."

"I was given this number by your Aunt Lucy."

"How can I help?"

"My name is Tuppence Farthing."

What a great name!

"I own the thimble shop in Candlefield. I don't know if you know it?"

"The Finger?"

"That's the one."

"I've never been in, but yes, I know where it is."

"We've had a spate of thefts recently. I've spoken to the police, but to be honest, they don't seem very interested in the theft of a few thimbles. But, it's rather important to me that we get it resolved. Your Aunt Lucy suggested that you might be able to help."

"Of course. Would you like me to pop in?"

"Please, if you could. We're busy stocktaking today, so perhaps tomorrow or the day after?"

"I'd be happy to."

Thimble theft? I got all the high profile cases.

***

I'd promised Ms Turtle that I'd go over to Middle

Tweaking. She was apparently going to show me everything she knew about being an investigator.

Snigger. Poor old dear.

I would no doubt have the murder solved in no time, but I'd be sure to do it in such a way as not to embarrass her. And, I'd obviously let her take some of the credit. I was big-hearted like that.

The drive to Middle Tweaking in daylight was most enjoyable. On my way there, I drove through Lower Tweaking. And from what Kathy had told me, I understood there was a Higher Tweaking on the other side of Middle Tweaking. Lots of Tweaking going on, apparently.

Middle Tweaking was picture postcard beautiful — complete with village green and duck pond. It was exactly what you'd expect of the English countryside. There were no identikit high street shops to be found. Next door to The Old Trout was the butcher's shop, and on the other side was the post office where the murder had taken place. On the opposite side of the street was a fishmonger, a pharmacy, and what appeared to be a small souvenir shop. A village like that would no doubt attract its fair share of tourists. The houses, including several thatched cottages, were all very quaint.

There was a young woman with a pram, walking down the street. I asked if she could give me directions to the old watermill.

"Ah, you're looking for Myrtle."

"Ms Turtle, yes."

"You need to carry on straight through the village. The old watermill is on the right. You can't miss it. It's a large grey building."

I thanked the woman, and drove on down the road. Sure enough, the old watermill was unmistakable. I parked my car next to an old Morris Minor, which I assumed belonged to Ms Turtle. But she'd come to Washbridge on the bus, so perhaps she was a little too old to drive now?

There was a large brass knocker on the door. When I pulled it back and released it, a thunderous noise seemed to echo through the building. A few moments later, I heard footsteps, and the door creaked open. It was Myrtle Turtle; she was wearing a blue cardigan, a tweed skirt and slippers.

"Ah, it's you, young lady. I wasn't sure if you'd come. So few young people are reliable these days."

"I hope it's convenient, Ms Turtle."

"Do come in."

The interior was not what I'd been expecting. The furnishings were all very modern—not a rocking chair in sight.

"I'll just turn this down." She took a smartphone from her pocket, and used it to stop the music.

"How did you do that, Ms Turtle?"

"It's Spotify Connect. I have it in all the rooms."

Spotify? Smartphones? Maybe, I'd misjudged this old girl?

"I usually listen to vinyl."

"You're really behind the times, aren't you, young lady?"

Ms Turtle made tea for us both. Earl Grey, and very nice it was, too. Even better, she got the sugar measure precisely right.

"Would you care for a biscuit, Jill?"

"What do you have?"

"I have a variety, but I like to keep them all separate." She opened a cupboard inside which were several Tupperware containers. "I have bourbons, rich tea, chocolate digestives and custard creams."

"Custard creams for me, please."

"They're my second favourite. I prefer the bourbons."

That was just wrong, but I didn't feel it was my place to comment.

"I like to keep my biscuits in separate containers too," I said.

"Really? There's hope for you yet."

Over tea, we got chatting, and she began to let her guard down a little.

"Ms Turtle, what did you used to do before you retired, if you don't mind my asking?"

"You can ask, Jill, but if I told you, I'd be forced to kill you." She laughed.

I laughed too, but there was something in the way she'd said it that made me wonder if there wasn't at least a grain of truth in it. Was she ex-police, ex-forces or something more sinister?

"What about the local police, Ms Turtle? Don't they object to you getting involved with their investigations?"

"They're not exactly thrilled, but they tend to put up with it because I've been doing it for so long. Besides which, this is not the city. The police have to cover all of the Tweakings, and several other villages. That leaves them spread rather thin. It helps that my track record is rather good. What about you? Do you have any problems with the police in Washbridge?"

"I used to—with one detective in particular."

"And you don't now? Has he moved to a different region?"

"Actually, he's now my boyfriend."

"That's one way to get someone on your side, I suppose." She smiled. "Drink up and we'll get cracking."

We'd no sooner stepped out of the door than we ran into a police officer; his face lit up when he spotted Ms Turtle.

"Hello, Myrtle."

"Charlie. Can I introduce you to this young lady? Her name is Jill Gooder. She's a private investigator from Washbridge."

"Pleased to meet you, young lady." Charlie Cross had a winning smile, and a firm handshake. He looked old enough to have retired himself.

"Nice to meet you too, Sergeant."

"None of that Sergeant nonsense. Everyone around here calls me Charlie."

"Okay, Charlie."

"What brings you to Middle Tweaking, Jill?"

"I was at The Old Trout the other night for the murder mystery."

"I see. It's tragic what happened to Madge. Did you know it was to be the last murder mystery evening?"

"I think the landlord mentioned it."

"The players had some kind of falling out, and decided they could no longer work together, but they honoured their remaining bookings."

"I thought at the time they didn't seem very happy. They didn't appear to be into what they were doing."

"They were probably just going through the motions.

I'm still not sure why you're back in Middle Tweaking, though."

Ms Turtle interrupted. "Jill's here to learn, Charlie. I promised that she could work alongside me while I investigate this one."

"I suppose I'd be wasting my breath if I told you that neither of you should get involved?"

"You would."

"I won't bother then." He'd obviously had this same conversation with Ms Turtle a thousand times before.

"He seems like a nice chap, Ms Turtle."

"Why are you calling me Ms Turtle?"

"You told me to."

"I'm sure I didn't. Call me Myrtle."

Huh?

"Okay, Myrtle. I was just saying that Charlie seems nice."

"He is. In fact, there was a time when he and I were — close."

"I *thought* he looked pleased to see you."

"We saw each other for a short while, but it didn't work out for one reason or another. But, we've remained firm friends since then."

I couldn't help but wonder if that's what would happen with Jack and me.

"Okay, Jill, you're supposed to be the private investigator. Tell me, where would you normally start with a case such as this?"

I hadn't been expecting her to put me on the spot like that.

"Ideally with the murder scene, but I don't imagine we'll be allowed in there."

"We won't, but I just happen to have a 'contact' inside the force."

"A contact?"

"I can't be any more specific. I have to protect my sources. The long and short of it is that I have photographs of the murder scene." She reached inside her handbag and passed me two photographs.

In the first, Madge Hick was lying dead in the kitchen. The second was a close-up of the kitchen floor which was covered in what looked like flour. Before she died, Madge had been able to write two letters in the flour: 'FL'.

"Any idea what the letters stand for?"

"Florence Long is the obvious answer, but somehow I can't picture Florence as a murderer."

"Was there any sign of a forced entry?"

"None. Either she knew her killer, and let him in, or someone had sneaked through the post office into her flat while the shop was busy."

"Do you know the cause of death?"

"Officially no, but the pathologist, Henry Twoshank, is a good friend of mine. We play croquet sometimes."

"Croquet? Isn't that deadly boring?"

"Absolutely, but I get a lot of my leads from there. According to Henry, Madge was poisoned, but he hasn't yet been able to identify the specific poison. She also had a small puncture wound on the side of her neck."

"Are the two things related?"

"Possibly."

"That's very interesting, but it doesn't get us very far."

"I agree. What would you do next, Jill?"

"Well, obviously I'd like to speak to the other murder mystery players."

"I agree, but to do that I'll need to arrange interviews with each of them."

"Couldn't we just doorstep them?"

"Not as a first resort. We'll try the polite way first. I'll give you a call when I've managed to arrange something, then we can conduct the interviews together."

# Chapter 6

Jack phoned. Maybe after enduring a night out with Kathy, he'd decided he wanted to call it a day. Who could blame him?

"Hey, petal—sorry—I mean Jill. Look, it's just a thought, but I wondered if you'd like to go to that new bar in town. Have you seen it? Bar Fish? Weird kind of a name."

Not only had I heard of it, I'd actually been there on a couple of occasions. But I didn't want to spoil Jack's surprise, so I played along.

"Bar Fish? I don't think I know it."

"Apparently, they've got tropical fish everywhere. It gets very good reviews. I thought we could go there tonight, if you're not doing anything. It would be nice to have an evening when it's just you and me—no Miles and Mindy, no Kathy and Peter. What do you say? Are you free?"

"That sounds great. Shall I meet you there?"

"Yeah. That's probably best. Let's say eight o' clock. I should be done by then, barring a major incident."

"Eight's fine by me."

"Do you know where it is?"

"I'll find it."

Well, well! This was beginning to look like a real relationship.

I had to pay a visit to the print-shop because I'd run out of business cards. I'd no sooner stepped out of my office when someone tapped me on the shoulder. It was my *bestest* friend, Miles Best.

"What do you want, Miles?"

"Jill, I'm glad I bumped into you."

"Looks like you were following me."

"You're right. I've been waiting for you to come out."

Normally, Miles was all smiles, but today he looked subdued—worried even.

"Jill, I need a favour."

I laughed. "That is a joke, right?"

"No, I'm serious."

"You're asking me for a favour after that ad campaign you ran?"

"I'm really sorry about that. I meant no harm."

"Of course you didn't. Like you didn't mean any harm when you put the rats in Cuppy C."

"That was only a joke."

"I don't believe you. You were trying to get Cuppy C closed down."

"I would never do anything like that. I still have a soft spot for the twins."

"You have a funny way of showing it."

"I know, and I'm sorry. But it really was just meant as a bit of fun. I've always liked playing practical jokes."

"It's time you grew up, then."

"You're right, and I will, I promise. But I really do need a favour."

"I'm listening."

"It's your grandmother."

"What about her?"

"I guess you already know that she's sabotaged my wool subscription service."

"I know no such thing. How do you know it isn't just broken?"

"Come on, Jill. You know as well as I do that your grandmother is behind it."

"If she is, and I'm not saying she is, but if she is, why are you talking to me?"

"She won't listen to anything I've got to say."

"It sounds like you're kind of stuffed then."

"Please, Jill. This is really serious. I realise that we may have overstepped the mark a little."

"A *little*?"

"Okay, a lot then. But Mindy is really keen on this wool shop. It's something that she's always wanted to do, and now it looks like we're going to be closed down before we even get started. If things carry on like they are, we'll be bankrupt."

"I still don't know what you expect *me* to do about it."

"Would you have a word with your grandmother, and ask her to reverse the spell which is causing the wool subscription to fail?"

"Why should I do that?"

"What if I promise to close down Best P.I. Services?"

"Close it down? Do you actually have any clients yet?"

"No, but we soon will have after all the advertising we've done. If you could get your grandmother to take back the spell, I'll give up Best P.I. Services."

"And do you promise that there'll be no more dirty tricks on either Cuppy C or Ever A Wool Moment?"

"You have my word."

"Your word? Oh well. That's okay then."

"I mean it, Jill. I'll close Best P.I. Services today if you get your grandmother to reverse the spell."

He looked so desperate that I couldn't help but feel a little sorry for him. I'd certainly be glad to see the back of

Best P.I. Services. I didn't need any more competition.

"Okay. I'll talk to Grandma, but I can't promise she'll listen."

"Thank you, Jill." He threw his arms around me, and gave me a hug.

"Get off!" I pushed him away.

"Sorry. And, thanks again."

"Are you sure that you only need two-hundred of these?" The man behind the counter at the print-shop had a smudge of ink under his nose. It looked like some kind of weird, blue moustache.

"Yeah. Two-hundred will be fine."

"I only ask because most people order a minimum of a thousand."

Most people probably have clients to give them to. I still had some of the last batch, but they'd yellowed with age.

"Two hundred is fine, thanks."

"What does P.I. stand for? Is it Pet's Insurance?"

Oh boy. Why did I always get them?

"Didn't you see the picture of a magnifying glass on the card?"

"Yeah, I did. I assumed that was something you use to help see the smaller pets better."

"You're right. That's exactly what it is. It's called a small pet maximiser."

He smiled—obviously pleased with himself. "I told Derek that's what it stood for. He thought it was Pottery Inspector. What an idiot."

Kathy was behind the counter at Ever A Wool Moment: she looked half asleep.

"I can see you're busy."

She yawned. "It's been dead in here all day. What about you? Are you busy?"

"Run off my feet, as always."

"Liar. How's Jack?"

"Okay, I think. I haven't seen or heard from him since the murder mystery evening," I lied. "I think you might have scared him off."

"Don't be ridiculous. He obviously enjoyed our company. We should do it again some time, the four of us."

"Yeah, we should. Some time." Like the twelfth of never. "Is Grandma in today?"

"In the back as usual."

"Don't fall asleep while I'm with her."

"Grandma, do you have a minute?"

"I always have a minute for one of my favourite grandchildren."

"Aren't I your favourite?"

"You're in the top three."

She seemed uncharacteristically jolly. Maybe this was a good time to ask her about Miles. Or maybe, she was just lulling me into a false sense of security.

"I wanted to ask you a favour."

"You *always* want to ask me a favour, Jill."

"I've just been talking to Miles Best. They're having a really bad time of it over there at Best Wool."

"Really? How very sad. Pass me a tissue."

"No. Listen. It sounds really serious. If they can't get things resolved before the end of the week, they'll probably go bankrupt."

"And I'm supposed to care about that, why?"

"Because I know deep down, you're a caring, compassionate person."

She laughed.

"Okay, maybe not. But surely, you can give him one more chance."

"Why doesn't the coward come over here himself, and ask me to reverse the spell?"

"He's probably scared of you."

"Of me? Why would anybody be scared of little old me?"

"I wonder."

"Do you know your problem, Jill?"

"I suspect you're about to tell me."

"You're too soft. You have to learn to be more ruthless. People will walk all over you, otherwise."

"He's promised to close down Best P.I. Services if you reverse the spell."

"Ah, now I get the picture. There was I thinking you were being soft, when in fact you were just looking after your own self-interests. That's my girl!"

"No, yes. I mean—I think it would be the right thing for you to do."

"Let me get this straight. You want me to back off *my* competition, so that Miles Best will close down Best P.I. Services, which will help *you*? That doesn't seem equitable. What do I get out of the deal?"

"My gratitude."

"What good is that to me? I can't spend gratitude."

"How about if I owe you a favour?"

What was I doing? Grandma's favours nearly always involved her feet.

"A favour? Hmm? Well, that's different."

"So? Is it a deal?"

"You can tell Miles that his wool will be working before the end of the day, but warn him that he'd better never bad-mouth Ever A Wool Moment again or he'll regret it."

"Thanks, Grandma. I'll tell him."

\*\*\*

I'd promised to visit The Finger, which was a small thimble shop near the market square in Candlefield. A chime rang as I walked through the door. The interior was delightful; all of the shelves were full of thimbles. It was absolutely charming.

"Hello." The squeaky little voice came from the back of the shop. It was the same squeaky little voice that had spoken to me on the phone.

"Hello there," I called, but I still couldn't see anyone.

Then, a tiny elf jumped onto the stool behind the counter.

"Are you Jill Gooder?"

"That's right. I promised I'd pop in today."

"Thanks for coming. I'm Tuppence Farthing."

"Nice to meet you, Tuppence. What is it I can do for you exactly?"

"Over the last three or four weeks, we've had several thimbles stolen."

"When you say 'several', how many are we talking about?"

"At least forty. They didn't all disappear in one go. It tends to be one or two at a time."

"I see. And you haven't seen who's taking them?"

"No. That's the strange thing. The only time we've noticed they were missing is at the end of the day when we've been closing up."

"Can you think of anyone who'd want to steal your thimbles?"

"Not really. They're very pretty, but they're not particularly valuable. We've been open for years, and I honestly don't remember there being any thefts before."

"Is there anything else you can tell me that might help? Has anything unusual happened recently?"

"The strange thing is, all the thimbles that have disappeared have had pictures of cottages on them. We have all sorts of designs in the shop: animals, landscapes, toys, seashells — all sorts of things."

"That doesn't sound like a coincidence."

"It can't be. It's as though someone has stolen them to order."

"And you say you've reported this to the police?"

"Yes, I've spoken to them, but they weren't interested. They said they'd send someone round, but that was weeks ago and they still haven't been. I think we can safely assume they're not coming."

"Okay, Tuppence, I'll see what I can find out, and I'll get back to you."

"Thank you so much, Jill."

*** 

Even though I was running five minutes early, Jack was already waiting outside Bar Fish when I arrived.

"You must have got away early," I said, as he gave me a peck on the cheek.

"Yeah. It was pretty quiet, so I thought I'd make a break for it before anything else came in. Have you seen this place?" He pointed through the window. "Look at that wall; it's absolutely full of tropical fish. And behind the bar, there are tubes running along the back. Even under the floor; look at those tanks."

"It looks fantastic."

"Come on then." He took my hand. "Let's go inside."

"What are you drinking, Jill? White wine?"

"They don't do wine; they only serve fishtails."

Whoops!

He gave me a puzzled look. "How do you know that?"

"I—err—I—saw an article in The Bugle about the opening. It said they'd only be serving their version of cocktails—called fishtails."

"Ah, right. Clever gimmick."

"Hello again," the barman said. "You're becoming a regular."

Oh bum!

Jack looked even more puzzled.

"I have that kind of a face. People are always mistaking me for someone else."

Now it was the barman's turn to look confused.

"I'll go get us a table, Jack. You can order for me."

Phew! I'd got away with it—just!


We'd been in there for about an hour. The conversation was flowing freely; the fish were a delight. In fact, everything was going swimmingly.

What? Come on, you must have seen that one coming.

"Hello there, Jack. How's it going?" A thick-set man, with more teeth than was healthy, approached us. "And who's this delightful young lady?"

"Hi, Stuart. This is Jill Gooder."

"Welcome to Bar Fish, Jill. I'm Stuart Steele. I own this place."

"Pleased to meet you."

"I assume you've taken advantage of the comp tickets I dropped off at the station, Jack?"

Comp tickets? So *that's* why he'd wanted to go to Bar Fish; he'd got tickets for free drinks. The cheapskate.

"What do you do, Jill? Are you a police officer too?"

"No. I'm a private investigator."

"Really? How fascinating. Well look, I'm sure the two of you would rather be alone, so I'll leave you to it."

After he'd gone, I turned to Jack. "Comp tickets? Free drinks?"

"Didn't I mention that?"

"You know you didn't." I laughed. "No wonder you were so keen to go out tonight. I didn't realise you were such a cheapskate."

"Busted. Apparently Stuart's hoping to franchise this concept. If this place takes off, he plans to open similar bars around the country."

"Based on what I've seen so far I'd say he's in with a good chance. It's a novel idea, and people certainly seem to like it."

By nine-thirty, the place was becoming crowded, and we were struggling to hear ourselves think. But then, all of a sudden, the noise was pierced by a loud scream. All eyes turned to a woman, who was pointing at the floor.

"Stay here," Jack said.

I ignored him, and followed as he pushed his way through the crowd. When we reached the woman, she was hysterical, and was still pointing to the floor. Floating in the tank under the floor, was a young woman's body; her dead eyes stared up through the glass. It was a face I recognised. A face I'd seen on the front page of The Bugle. It was Starr Fish — the reality TV celebrity.

Jack flashed his warrant card, made a call to the station, and then addressed the crowd.

"Stand back, please. I'm Detective Maxwell. No one leaves until my colleagues arrive, and they've had a chance to take your names and addresses."

Another uneventful date drew to a close.

# Chapter 7

My phone rang; it was Myrtle.

"Jill, look, I'm sorry about this, but the murder mystery players are being rather awkward. I'd hoped to arrange for us to interview them all on the same day, but it seems that's not going to be possible. We're going to have to spread it over a few days. I can't really expect you to travel back and forth from Washbridge, so I'll understand if you can't make it, but I thought I should at least let you know what was happening."

"I'd still like to be involved, Myrtle, if that's okay with you."

"Are you sure? It's such a long way to come."

"I'm absolutely positive."

It wasn't as though I had any work of a meaningful nature. I could hardly class the thimbles theft as a major case. And besides, that was in Candlefield, so time would stand still in Washbridge while I was over there.

"Very well, dear. I've set up the first interview with Florence Long tomorrow at three-fifteen. Can you make it then?"

"I'll be there. Should I meet you at your place?"

"Yes, we'll go over to her house from there."

\*\*\*

My relationship with Jack had been weighing heavy on my mind, so I'd called Love Spell and spoken to Hilary. She'd said I could drop by their Washbridge office, to have a chat.

It was a while since I'd been there; Nathaniel was still

working on reception. He greeted me with a welcoming smile, and asked me to take a seat. Moments later, Hilary popped her head out of her office, and called me through.

"Thanks for seeing me at such short notice, Hilary."

"It's the least I can do. We owe you a lot, Jill. If it hadn't been for your help, we probably wouldn't have a business right now. What exactly is it I can help you with? Surely, you're not looking for a partner? I'd heard on the grapevine that you're dating that sexy policeman."

"Yes, Jack and I are seeing each other, and no, I'm not looking for a date."

"How can I help, then?"

"It's about my relationship with Jack. I knew going in that sups were not allowed to reveal themselves to humans, but I never really appreciated what that meant in practice. Well, I guess I did to a certain extent because I've had to hide it from my sister and her husband, and from Mrs V, who I work with. But, being in a relationship with someone makes it way more difficult. How are you supposed to live with someone when you're not able to tell that person exactly who you are?"

"Are you and Jack living together now?"

"No, but we certainly see a lot more of one another than we used to. Living together will probably be the next step, but that scares me. It doesn't feel right to enter into a relationship with someone knowing full well that you'll always have to keep secrets from them. It struck me that you must come across this dilemma all the time. Presumably every witch who goes through your books has to face this problem."

"You're right, they do. And I wish I could tell you that there's an easy solution, but I'd be lying. It's difficult for all of our witches. Some of them handle it better than others. Some can keep that part of their life secret from their partner, and not feel any guilt. Others struggle. Many of them have sat exactly where you're sitting right now, and said much the same as you've just said."

"Have you been able to help them?"

"I'm not sure that I have, to be honest. The best situation is one where a witch has no family in Candlefield because then there's less to hide. Where a witch does have family, it's much more difficult because, inevitably, she'll want to keep in touch with them. Juggling both 'lives' is not easy."

"Surely things must go wrong occasionally? There must be instances where a witch has done or said something that's given her away?"

"It does happen. There's no question about that."

"What happens in such instances?"

"It all depends. If the transgression comes to the attention of the powers-that-be in Candlefield, then it's quite likely they'll send a Rogue Retriever to bring back the witch. That would basically be the end of the relationship."

"That's terrible. What happens to the husband in such cases?"

"That's the real tragedy. They'll have no idea where their wife went. They'll most likely report her as missing to the police, and may even try to convince them that she's a witch. If they do that, the police are likely to write the husband off as a nutter. It's a terrible state of affairs all around."

"You said *if* the transgression gets back to the powers-that-be. Does that mean sometimes it doesn't?"

"I can't be sure. I suspect that there are a few cases where the husband finds out his wife is a witch, but where they're able to keep a lid on it. That can only happen if their relationship is strong enough to withstand such a shock, and if the husband is capable of keeping their secret. I'd be very surprised if there aren't at least a few couples who fall into that category, but that's pure speculation."

Although Hilary hadn't been able to offer me a 'magic pill' to resolve my dilemma, she had at least given me something to think about. It had never occurred to me that there might be couples living happily in Washbridge where the husband knew his wife was a witch.

***

I was on my way back to the office, and had just walked into the building when I bumped into Armi.

"Hello there, Jill. You're looking exceptionally beautiful today, I must say. I've just been chatting with Annabel. She's in jolly good form, and that blue hair of hers is absolutely delightful, don't you think?"

"Err—yes—it's very nice."

The quiet, little, *wouldn't say boo to a goose* man had been transformed into *Mr Self-Confidence*. It appeared my spell had done the trick.

"I can't stop, Jill. I have a couple of errands to run. I'll catch up with you and Annabel later. Too-da-loo."

"Too-da-loo, Armi."

My goodness.

Mrs V looked in a state of shock. "Did you see him,

Jill?"

"Armi? Yes."

"Whatever happened to him? He's like a different man. He came in here, complemented me on my hair, and then planted a huge kiss on my lips." She half blushed/half smiled.

"He's a bit of a dark horse, isn't he? Do you like the new Armi?"

"I'm not sure. I haven't had time to think about it yet. I'm still in shock."

"Well, at least now he'll be able to stand up to Gordon."

"I suppose so. That's a good thing, at least."

When I walked into my office, it was like deja vu. The small dining table was back, and had been set for a meal. Winky was busy polishing the cutlery.

"Are you entertaining Katrina again?"

"Definitely not. I couldn't put up with that a second time. I'm still having nightmares about the noises she made when she ate."

"What's this then? Are you expecting another candidate from Purrfect Match?"

"If you must know, Bella is coming over tonight."

"She is?"

"I've given the matter serious consideration, and I've come to the conclusion that Socks was to blame. Bella should have known better, but my brother can be very persuasive. He's always been a bit of a ladies' man. I've decided to give her the benefit of the doubt, and another chance."

"That's very magnanimous of you."

"I know. I'm a fool to myself sometimes."

"I'm really pleased. You and Bella make such a lovely couple."

"Don't get carried away, Jill. It's only dinner. Now, if you'll excuse me, I have a lot to prepare."

I could have objected to my office being taken over yet again, but I was so pleased that Winky and Bella were back together, I decided to go home early, and leave him to his preparations.

Back at my flat, I'd been waylaid by Mr Ivers.

"I'm glad I've bumped into you, Jill."

That makes one of us.

"You and I are the only people in this building who aren't terminally boring," he said.

Huh?

"Take that Betty Longbottom, for example. All she's interested in, is crustaceans and the likes. It's enough to drive you insane."

"Betty's okay."

Why was I sticking up for the tax inspecting, jelly fish wielding little minx?

"And then there's Luther Stone. Since he's taken up with Betty, all he wants to talk about is sea creatures. It's like she's got him under a spell. I sometimes wonder if she's a witch."

"You might have something there."

"The two of them cornered me earlier today." Mr Ivers shook his head. "I had stereo crustaceans coming at me. It was horrible."

"You're right. There's nothing worse than being trapped by someone intent on boring you to death."

"Precisely. Anyway, you'll be pleased to hear that I've

just finished this month's newsletter."

Oh irony, thou art a cruel neighbour.

He was still talking—apparently. "I'm waiting for my new toner cartridge to arrive, so I can print them off. But, don't worry. I'll get the next issue to you PDQ."

"PDQ? Great. IDNC." I. Do. Not. Care.


I'd made myself macaroni and cheese. It was all I could be bothered with, but it hit the mark. I was enjoying the last few mouthfuls when the room became a little chilly, and my mother appeared.

"Is that *all* you're having to eat, Jill?"

"It's what I fancied."

"It's hardly a meal, is it? With all the stresses and strains your job entails, you need more than macaroni and cheese."

"Have you come here just to nag me?"

"That's a mother's job."

"You didn't nag me for the first twenty odd years of my life."

"No, but I wanted to when I saw some of the things you got up to."

"Was there another reason for your visit today? Other than to criticise my diet?"

"Actually, I wanted to tell you how pleased I am that you and Jack are seeing more of one another."

"And you know that, how?"

"A mother knows these things."

"In other words, you've been following us."

"Of course not."

"So you weren't at The Old Trout the other day?"

She laughed. "You made a bit of a fool of yourself at

that murder mystery—whoops—err—I mean—no, I wasn't there."

"Mum, what have I told you? I don't want you looking over my shoulder all the time."

"No. Obviously, but I do think that this man is a good catch, so don't go doing anything stupid, again."

"What do you mean *again*?"

"You have a bad habit of opening your mouth before your brain has engaged."

"Thanks! "

"Sorry. I'll keep my nose out."

"That's the most sensible thing you've said since you got here."

"Okay, I'll go. I know when I'm not wanted."

"Wait! There is something I'd like to ask you."

"Are you sure? I wouldn't want to stick my nose in."

"Touché. I've been giving a lot of thought to how a relationship between a witch and a human might work. Relationships should be based on trust and honesty, but if I was to be with Jack, I wouldn't be able to tell him that I'm a witch. Effectively, I'd be lying to him."

"That's just how it is, unless you take another sup as a partner."

"Someone suggested that there are relationships between witches and humans where the husband *does* know his wife is a witch, but because he's able to keep that a secret, they're able to carry on without any interference from Candlefield."

"Who's this *someone* who's been advising you?"

"I'd rather not say."

"I'd call that very bad advice. Such a relationship would be fraught with danger. A wrong word at the wrong time, and the next thing you know, the Rogue Retrievers would be called into action, and that would be the end of the marriage."

"I guess you're right. Okay, thanks."

Not long after my mother had disappeared, my phone rang. I didn't recognise the man's voice.

"Is that Jill Gooder?"

"Speaking."

"It's Stuart Steele. We met in Bar Fish."

"Yes, Stuart. I'm sorry about what happened yesterday."

"Me too. It was a terrible thing. That's why I'm calling, actually. I wondered whether you'd be prepared to come and see me. I need someone to find out exactly what happened."

"Surely the police are doing that?"

"Yes, but based on past experience, I'm not convinced that things will move as quickly as I need them to. If this isn't cleared up soon, it could be very bad for my plans to franchise the business. Would you at least be prepared to come to my house to talk to me?"

I hesitated. I knew what Jack would say if he found out I was involved.

"Sure. Give me your address, and I'll come over there tomorrow."

# Chapter 8

"Jill, I'm really worried," Mrs V said, as soon as I walked into the office the next morning.

"What's happened now?"

"It's Armi."

"Is he okay?"

"Yeah, no. I don't know. You remember I told you he came in yesterday, and gave me a kiss?"

"Yeah?"

"Well, he's just done it again. He came bursting in, kissed me, and asked me to go to Paris for the weekend."

"Wow! Did you say you'd go?"

"I think so. It all happened so quickly."

"That's great, isn't it? Paris is lovely at this time of year."

"I know. I really want to go, but I can't figure out what's happened to Armi. Last week I could barely get two words out of him. He was so shy, quiet, and reserved, but now he's like a man possessed."

"Maybe that's the effect you have on him, Mrs V."

"Don't be ridiculous, Jill. Something's happened. Do you think he's on drugs or something?"

"Armi? No, he's not the kind of man to take drugs. Maybe being with you has given him the confidence he's always been missing."

"Do you really think so?"

"Definitely." Or maybe not.

*** 

It was a while since I'd seen Aunt Lucy, so I magicked

myself over to her house where I found her sitting at the kitchen table. She looked down in the dumps; it looked as though there were tears in her eyes.

"Aunt Lucy, are you okay?"

"Sorry, Jill. I didn't realise you were here. Yes, I'm fine." She wiped her eyes. "Would you like a cup of tea?"

"It's okay. I'll make one for both of us. You stay where you are."

I made tea, put a few custard creams on a plate, and joined her at the kitchen table.

"Aunt Lucy, I know something's wrong." I put my hand on hers. "What is it? Is it Lester?"

"No dear. Everyone's all right. It's not the family; it's just me being silly."

"About what?"

"This article." She pushed a newspaper towards me.

"Homeless Fairies?"

"It's so sad. Have you come across the starlight fairies before?"

"I don't think so."

"They're delightful little people. They're the tiniest sups in Candlefield—the size of a pinhead. Their population has exploded over recent years, but housing for them hasn't kept pace, and now lots of them are homeless."

"I always thought fairies lived in the woods."

"In the human world, maybe, but here in Candlefield they normally live in houses like the rest of us. A friend of mine, Diane Bayswater, runs FairyAid, a charity which is trying to help them. She's asked if I'll help out."

"Raising funds?"

"I suppose so. I'm going to meet with her in the next couple of days to see what she'd like me to do."

"If there's anything I can do, let me know."

"That's very generous, Jill, but I think you've already done enough with your work for SupAid."

***

I hadn't told Jack that I was going to see Stuart Steele. He wouldn't have been very happy if he'd known, but I had a business to run, and a living to earn.

I arrived at Stuart's house ten minutes before the time we'd agreed. It was a large house, and had obviously cost a pretty penny. As I arrived, a tow-truck, with the name Beeline Motors and the logo of a cute bee driving a car, was picking up a black four-by-four from in front of the house.

Stuart answered the door. "Jill, thank you very much for coming." He must have seen me glance at the car. "They're taking it in for repair; it packed up on me yesterday."

"Mine broke down the other day in the middle of nowhere. If it hadn't been for Malcolm the mobile barber, I would have been in a real pickle."

"Mobile barber?"

"Yes, he's a funny little guy. He has a mobile barber shop which he insists on parking in the middle of nowhere."

"How does he get customers?"

"He doesn't; at least, not many. But he seems happy enough, so who are we to question him?"

"Let's go through to the living room."

There were fish tanks embedded in the walls of the corridors, and in the living room was a large open-topped tank with glass steps leading up to it.

"Fascinating aren't they?" he said. "Would you like to feed them?"

"No, thanks. I take it this is a hobby of yours?"

"It is indeed — ever since I was a child. My father bought my first fish tank for me when I was six years old, and it grew from there. I eventually started my own shop — you may have seen it: Something Fishy. It's in Washbridge, close to the library."

"I can't say I have."

"Bar Fish is the next step in my plan for world fish domination. If it's successful, I hope to sell franchises. Hopefully, you'll soon see a Bar Fish in cities throughout the country." He frowned. "Of course, after last night, things aren't looking quite so rosy."

"Did you know Starr Fish?"

"I'm not really a fan of reality TV, but you'd have to be blind and deaf not to have heard of her. She was never off the front pages of the tabloids, and all over the internet. I'd heard that she'd disappeared, but that was as much as I knew about her."

"If you didn't know her, why would you want to spend money to find out who killed her?"

"Pure self-interest, I must confess. The longer this drags on, the worse it will be for Bar Fish. If it can be cleared up quickly, maybe I can still salvage something out of the situation. Would there be a problem with Jack if you were to take on the case?"

"Not a problem as such, but if it's all the same to you, I'd prefer not to mention it to him. I wouldn't want him to think I was treading on his toes."

"Absolutely. A nod is as good as a wink. I would like

you to give me regular updates though."

"Of course."

***

As I walked past the newsagent, I noticed The Bugle's front page, and couldn't believe what I was seeing. I'd thought The Bugle had already plunged the depths of gutter journalism, but this took it to a whole new sordid level. The photo on the front page was of Starr Fish in the tank at Bar Fish. Her dead eyes seemed to be staring through the glass at the lens of the camera. How could anyone publish that? How would her family feel when they saw it? It made my blood boil.

I rushed straight over to their offices, burst through reception, and made a beeline for Dougal Bugle's desk.

"If it isn't Jill Gooder. To what do we owe this pleasure?"

"This!" I waved a copy of The Bugle in his face.

"Did you come to congratulate me on another brilliant article?"

"How could you publish a photograph like this?"

"We're only reporting the news."

"You could have done that without the photo. What about her poor family? How do you think they'll feel when they see this?"

"I think they have bigger things to worry about. And besides, I don't see what it's got to do with you."

"I want to know who took this photo."

"I'm sorry, but that's confidential."

I grabbed him by the tie. "Tell me who took the photo, Dougal."

"If you don't let me go, I'll call the police. I'm sure Jack Maxwell would be interested to see what his girlfriend gets up to."

Before I could release Dougal, the guy at the next desk had snapped a photo of me. I was tempted to take the camera out of his hand, and smash it into pieces, but no doubt there'd be three more cameras taking photos of that too. The damage was already done. I needed to get out of there before I did anything else I'd regret.

"You're a disgrace, Dougal." I released him. "A worm."

My heart was still in overdrive after I'd left the building. Moments later, my phone rang. I had to take a deep breath to compose myself.

"Hello?"

"Jill? It's Susan Hall."

Susan Hall was The Bugle's newest recruit. She'd visited my office to introduce herself, and to tell me that she shared a lot of my concerns about that rag. She had hoped she'd be able to transform it into a more reputable publication. If today's events were anything to go by, it looked as though she'd failed miserably.

"Have you seen the front page of your publication, Susan?"

"I have. I think it's terrible."

"I thought you said you were going to clean up The Bugle."

"I'm working on it, but it's not going to happen overnight."

"That photo is beyond the pale."

"I agree. That's why I'm calling."

"What do you mean?"

"I saw you with Dougal. I was hoping you'd punch him

in the nose."

"I came very close."

"Look, you didn't hear this from me, but the photographer was George Pullman—he's a freelancer."

"Thanks, Susan."

Maybe there was hope for Susan Hall yet.

\*\*\*

It was time to make my way over to Middle Tweaking. I'd arranged to meet Myrtle at the old watermill.

"Ah, Jill. You came." Myrtle greeted me. "I wasn't sure if you would. Are you positive you want to do this?"

"Absolutely, yes."

"There is one piece of interesting information I've picked up since you were last here. It seems that the murder mystery players had a lottery syndicate going. They played the same numbers every week, and because Madge ran the post office where the lottery is sold, she was responsible for purchasing the tickets. Anyway, a few weeks ago now, it seems that their numbers came up. They didn't stand to win the jackpot, but they would have ended up with five thousand each. Not to be sniffed at. Unfortunately, it turned out that Madge had forgotten to buy the ticket that week, so they ended up with nothing.

She was understandably devastated to have let down her friends in that way. It seems that some of them accepted her apology, and understood it had been a genuine mistake. Others suggested that she'd *never* bought the tickets, and had pocketed the money every week assuming that they'd never win, so no one would be any the wiser."

"Presumably there was a lot of bad feeling in the group."

"Yes. Some were annoyed with Madge; others were annoyed with those who refused to believe it had been a genuine mistake. That's undoubtedly why they'd decided to abandon the murder mystery evenings." Myrtle grabbed her handbag. "Anyway, come on, we'd better get a move on. I've arranged for us to see Florence Long who runs the pharmacy."

Florence Long had a beautiful thatched cottage just outside the village. Myrtle and I found her waiting for us on the front porch.

"Myrtle, nice to see you again."

"And you, Florence. How are you keeping?"

"My arthritis is playing up a little at the moment. It's the weather, I think." She turned to me. "Who is this young lady?"

"This is Jill Gooder. She was in the audience for the final murder mystery evening."

"I'm afraid I don't take much notice of the audience. I get very nervous, so I tend to focus on the lights."

"Jill works as a private investigator in Washbridge."

"I see. Would you both like a drink?"

Florence provided us with cold, hand-squeezed lemonade.

"Florence," Myrtle said. "How long had you and Madge known each other?"

"Madge and I have always been friends. We both grew up in Middle Tweaking; we went to school together. Lifelong friends, you could say."

"And what did you make of this lottery business?"

"The way Madge was treated was disgusting. She would no more cheat her friends than she'd steal money from the post office. The suggestion was preposterous. It was obvious that she genuinely forgot; she was devastated. We were all upset; it was a lot of money. But these things happen. Forgive and forget, I say, but some of the others didn't see it that way. That was the beginning of the end for the players."

"Was there anything else troubling Madge that you're aware of?"

"There was something, but I don't like to say."

"Come on, Florence. You know you can tell me anything."

"I know, Myrtle, but I wouldn't like it to get back to the police."

"I won't tell anyone, and Jill won't or I'd be forced to kill her." Myrtle grinned — she could be very scary when she wanted to be. "You won't tell anyone, will you, Jill?"

"My lips are sealed."

Florence took a deep breath. "I don't think it's common knowledge, but Madge had been seeing Brendan Breeze."

"Brendan? Really? You do surprise me. Brendan's a nice man, but he has a permanent smell of fish about him." Myrtle screwed up her nose.

"I know. I'm not sure how she put up with it. Apparently, they'd been seeing one another for some time, but then Brendan dropped her for his young assistant. By all accounts, Madge was heartbroken. She came to cry on my shoulder.

Shortly afterwards, I heard Brendan had accused Madge of taking her revenge by trying to sabotage his business. Absolutely ridiculous. Madge simply wasn't capable of such a spiteful act."

The three of us talked for another twenty minutes. Florence had many memories of Madge to recount, but none of them seemed particularly relevant to our investigation.

"What did you make of Florence?" Myrtle asked, as we walked back to the mill.

"She seemed harmless enough, but the Brendan Breeze connection might be worth looking at."

"Can you think of another reason to look more closely at Florence?" Myrtle pressed.

"I don't think so."

"Come on, Jill. It's obvious." Myrtle was beginning to remind me of Grandma and her tests.

"Not to me."

"The woman works in a pharmacy. She has ready access to all manner of drugs and poisons."

"But I thought the forensic people said they didn't recognise the poison."

"They did, but surely if anyone has the opportunity to mix chemicals and poisons together to produce something out of the ordinary, it would be a pharmacist. And then, there are the letters written in the flour."

"You're right, of course. I should have thought of that."

"Don't worry, Jill. We all have to start somewhere."

# Chapter 9

Mrs V was deep in thought when I walked into the office. So deep in thought, that she didn't even notice me come in.

"Mrs V?"

"Sorry, Jill. I was miles away."

"Everything okay?"

"I suppose so."

"It doesn't sound like it. What's the problem?"

"It's Armi. I don't know what to do about him."

"I thought you and he were going to Paris?"

"I don't think so. When I first met him, he was such a shy man; I couldn't help but like him. He isn't the same person now; he's just too much."

"I thought the change was for the better. Gordon had been giving him such a hard time. It was nice to see Armi grow in confidence, and be able to stick up for himself."

"It is, but I can't keep pace with him. He talks so much now that I can barely get a word in edgeways. And he's got all these ideas: we should do this, we should go there. It's all a bit too much for me. I think maybe it would be better if I called it off before things get out of hand."

"That would be such a shame. It might just be a temporary thing. Maybe he's taken some meds that don't agree with him. Look what happened to me when I took that hay fever medicine, and called him a goblin. Perhaps something like that caused his change in personality."

"Do you think so, Jill?"

"It's possible. Why don't you give it twenty-four hours, to see if he reverts to the Armi you used to know? If he doesn't, then you can call it a day. But at least give him the benefit of the doubt."

"You're right. I owe him that much at least. He's been so very kind to me; he even helped me with my Will. I'll give it twenty-four hours, as you say. But if he hasn't changed by then, I'm afraid that will be it."

Phew! I'd bought myself a little time, at least. Now, I needed to get to Armi, and reverse the spell which I'd cast on him. I'd better do it quickly otherwise Mrs V would call off their relationship, and then I'd feel terrible.

I told Mrs V that I had to go next door to Armitage, Armitage, Armitage and Poole to see Jules Rules about her employment paperwork. Jules seemed to be settling into her new role as receptionist quite nicely. Not bad for someone whose only previous experience had been packing black pudding and sausages.

"Hello, Jill," she said. "Can I help?"

"I'm here to see Joseph Armitage."

"Do you have an appointment?"

"No, but I'm sure you know that isn't going to stop me."

"But Jill, I might get in trouble if —"

"Sorry, Jules."

I started towards Armi's office, but before I got there, I heard a commotion coming from another office a few doors down. Gordon Armitage was arguing with Armi.

I crept over and peeked through the window. They didn't notice me because they were going at it hammer and tongs.

"I've told you, Joseph. I don't want you seeing that woman."

"It's none of your business, Gordon."

"I'm warning you, Joseph—"

"Which part of *none of your business* don't you understand?"

Armi was giving as good as he got. Go, Armi!

"I mean it, Joseph. I won't stand for it."

Armi walked up to his brother, grabbed his jacket lapels, and pinned him to the wall.

"I don't want to hear another word about it, Gordon. Do you understand? And, if you bad-mouth Annabel Versailles again, you'll have me to answer to."

Gordon Armitage looked both scared and confused. Little wonder. His older brother, Armi, who he'd been used to bullying, had finally turned on him.

I ducked into a vacant cubicle, and waited until Armi began to walk back to his own office. As he passed by, I reversed the spell. In a few minutes, he'd be back to the old Armi. Hopefully, that would mean Mrs V wouldn't have to break up with him. I doubted Gordon would cross Armi again any time soon because he'd be too afraid that he'd turn on him again.

\*\*\*

George Pullman, the freelance photographer who had taken the picture of Starr Fish, worked out of Maine House, which housed numerous small businesses— mainly start-ups and one-man bands.

The man who answered the door had thinning hair, and zero dress sense. Purple corduroy trousers had never been a good look.

"Can I help you?"

"I'm looking for George Pullman."

"That's me. I don't do wedding photography."

"I'm not here for wedding photography."

"Or christenings."

"I'm not here for that, either."

"I only do commercial and press."

"Funny you should say that because it's about press photography that I wanted to talk to you."

"What about it?"

"I understand from the people at The Bugle that you took the photograph of Starr Fish in the tank at Bar Fish."

"Who told you that?"

"Does it matter?"

"They specifically agreed that my name wouldn't be associated with that photograph."

"That'll teach you to trust anyone at The Bugle."

"Anyway, I don't have anything to say about it." He began to close the door, but I cast the 'power' spell, and pushed it open easily—knocking him backwards a few feet. Before he could react, I stepped into the room, and closed the door behind me.

"You have no right to come in here."

"You had no right to take photos of a dead woman, and then sell them to the newspapers."

"Starr Fish was a nasty piece of work."

"Even if that's true, she didn't deserve that. Anyway, what makes you say she was a nasty piece of work? Did you know her?"

"I lost my job because of her. I haven't always been freelance. I used to work for the Daily Gossip. She got in touch with me shortly before she went onto the reality TV show. She wanted me to take a photo of her—topless—she thought it would boost her ratings when she was in the house, and get her a few more votes."

"And did it?"

"Probably, but by the time it was published, she was already way ahead in the voting. She needn't have bothered with the topless photograph."

"I still don't understand why you lost your job?"

"She wanted me to take the photo through the bedroom window. She deliberately left the curtains open so I could do it. But then, when she won the show, she denied any knowledge of our arrangement. She accused me of invading her privacy, and I ended up getting the sack."

"It's quite a coincidence that you just happened to be at Bar Fish on the day that her body was found."

"It wasn't a coincidence at all. I was given a tip-off."

"That her body would be found there?"

"No, of course not. She'd been missing for a couple of days; the tip-off just said she'd be in that bar."

"Who did the tip-off come from?"

"I've no idea. I got a phone call out of the blue. I wasn't even sure whether to believe it, but I had nothing to lose, so I hung around Bar Fish hoping to catch a glimpse of her, and make a few bob from selling the photograph. The next thing I knew a woman was screaming blue murder. That's when I spotted Starr underneath the floor, so naturally I took a photo."

"Naturally. And then, *naturally*, you sold it to The Bugle."

"I offered it to a few other papers as well, but The Bugle made the best offer. I think some of the others were worried about publishing it."

"How do I know you didn't have something to do with Starr Fish's murder? You obviously had a grudge against her."

"I despised her, but I didn't kill her. Besides which, she had loads of enemies."

"What makes you say that?"

"Have you seen her autobiography? It's a real hatchet job."

"She has an autobiography?"

"She must have used a ghost-writer. I doubt Starr could spell the word 'autobiography'. You should read it. The murderer is most likely in there somewhere."

\*\*\*

I'd promised to meet Aunt Lucy at FairyAid because I wanted to see if there was anything I could do to help with the plight of the starlight fairies. En route, I called in at Cuppy C. The twins were dressed up, and looked like they were just off out.

"Hi, girls. Going out?"

"Unfortunately, yes," Amber said.

"Afraid so," Pearl said.

"Wow! You both look really enthusiastic, I must say. Where are you going?"

"To watch BoundBall practice."

"BoundBall?" I laughed. "You two hate BoundBall."

"I know." Amber pulled a face like she'd just sucked on a lemon.

"So, how come you're going?"

"We don't have much choice." Pearl sighed. "The boys have us over a barrel."

"Alan and William? How come?"

"Ever since they discovered that we hadn't told them about the double wedding, they've made our lives a misery. They've come up with a list of things we have to do to prove we love them."

"And going to a BoundBall practice session is one of them?"

"Yep," Amber said.

"But I thought you had them wrapped around your little finger?"

Just then, Alan and William walked into the shop. They were laughing and joking with one another.

"Hi, boys," I said. "I understand you're taking the twins to BoundBall practice?"

"Yeah, we are." Alan grinned. "Do you want to come too?"

"No thanks. I've had my share of BoundBall recently, but Amber and Pearl have just been telling me how much they're looking forward to it." I glanced at the twins, who were glaring back at me. "In fact, they said they'd love to go to every practice session, and all of the matches."

I don't know how I managed to keep a straight face. The twins looked as though they wanted to tear me limb from limb.

"Anyway, I can't stop. I've got to meet Aunt Lucy. See you."

I wouldn't be getting any free muffins for a while.

\*\*\*

FairyAid was based in modest offices near to the Town Hall. Aunt Lucy introduced me to Diane Bayswater, the lady in charge.

"Diane, this is my niece, Jill, who I told you about."

"Nice to meet you, Jill."

"I asked to come with Aunt Lucy to see if I can be of any help. I read the article about the plight of the starlight fairies; it's a tragedy."

"It really is, and yet so few people know about it. We have had one stroke of luck, though. We've recently managed to increase the output of new homes. In fact, we've got the latest batch in the back room, if you'd like to see them."

"You have houses in here?"

"Yes, but remember, we're talking about houses for fairies that are the size of a pinhead. The houses are barely bigger than your thumbnail."

"Of course, I should have realised. Yes, I'd love to see them."

"Follow me."

"I'll stay here," Aunt Lucy said. "I'll put some of these fliers together."

"There they are." Diane pointed to a table, on which was a tray full of small houses.

"Wow, those really are tiny."

"Would you like to see inside one?"

"Yes, please."

She took one gently between her thumb and finger, and tipped it on one side, so I could see inside. It was incredible — there were three small rooms, and stairs which I assumed led to the upper floor.

"May I?"

"Of course." She handed it to me. "Be careful; they're very fragile."

"The doors and windows are real."

"Of course. What did you expect?"

I was nervous of breaking something, so handed the

house back to Diane.

The houses were amazing, but they reminded me of something. Thimbles.

"Who makes these for you, Diane?"

"They're made by a goblin; a very talented man. There are very few people who can do this type of work, and his prices are very reasonable."

"What's his name?"

"Billy Somemates."

"Do you have an address for him? I'd love to see how he builds these."

"Yes, I'll let you have it before you leave."

*** 

When I got back to the office, I found Winky sitting in the windowsill. It was just like the good old days, watching him waving his little flags around. I crept up behind him, and looked across the way. Sure enough, there was Bella—returning his messages with her own tiny flags.

"I see you two are good again."

"I've decided to forgive her. We're making a new start, hence the semaphore."

Don't you just love a happy ending?

# Chapter 10

George Pullman, the photographer, might have been a sleaze bag, but if what he'd said about Starr Fish getting him sacked was true, he obviously had reason not to be her biggest fan. If nothing else, talking to him had made me aware of her autobiography. After I'd spoken to him, I bought a copy. By flicking through it, I soon managed to compile a short list of people who might harbour a grudge against her.

The first person I wanted to speak to was Starr's ex-boyfriend, a guy called Johnny Badger. Johnny lived locally in Washbridge; in fact, not too far from my own flat.

His hair was black with two white streaks running from front to back. Badger? Really?

"Mr Badger?"

"Are you the press?"

"No. My name is Jill Gooder. I'm a private investigator."

"Is this about Carol?"

The question threw me for a moment, but then I remembered that Starr Fish hadn't been born with that name. She used to be called Carol Smith, which I had to concede wasn't really a TV celebrity's name.

"Yes, Mr Badger, it's about Carol. Could I come in for a few moments, please?"

"Call me, Johnny. Yeah, come in. I'm afraid the place is a mess."

That was the understatement of the year. Dirty clothes had been dropped all over the floor and chairs. The sink was stacked high with dirty dishes. And, the place had obviously never seen a vacuum cleaner or a duster.

"Would you like a drink?"

At least the man had manners.

"No, thanks, I'm okay." I was actually parched, but I didn't want to risk a drink out of any of those cups. "How long had you and Carol been together before you broke up?"

"We didn't break up. She dumped me. We'd been together since high school; we were pretty much inseparable. I thought that we'd eventually get married. We'd even talked about it."

"Did you actually live together?"

"Yeah. She lived here with me for a couple of years. Then she saw that stupid advert in the paper."

"For the reality TV show?"

"Yeah. Life at the Top. We both decided to apply, just for a laugh. We didn't think we had a chance of getting on it because there'd be thousands applying. We both sent in an audition video. I shot Carol's, and she shot mine. Anyway, a bit later, I got an email saying 'Thanks, but no thanks', but Carol was asked to go in for an audition. Even then, we didn't think anything would come of it because there were still hundreds of people after only a few places on the show. But she got through the first round, and then the second round. By then, she was starting to get really excited. She kept talking about how it could make her a star. I humoured her, and hoped she wouldn't be too upset when they eventually turned her down. I even went with her for the final round of auditions. When they called her to say she was on the show, she was over the moon."

"How did you feel about it?"

"I made out that I was pleased, but really I was gutted, because I was worried it would change things between us. And it did. It changed everything, especially Carol."

"Is that when she changed her name?"

"Yes. It was a stupid idea. She said she couldn't go on the show with a name like Carol Smith—that no one would remember her. She didn't know what to change it to at first, but then one day, she told me she'd changed it to Starr Fish. I laughed because I thought it was a joke. She wasn't amused. After that, if I forgot, and called her Carol, she'd go mad at me."

"What happened when the show aired on TV?"

"Did you see it?"

"No, I don't watch much TV."

"It was extremely popular, and of course Carol stole the show. She went in there determined to do whatever it took to make sure she got noticed and voted for. She didn't seem to care what effect it might have on me."

"How do you mean?"

"She was flirting, and *more*, with all the guys on the show."

"And *more*?"

"Yes, if the tabloids are to be believed. She was on the front page of the papers every day with her antics. And, of course, she went on and won the whole thing."

"What happened between you two afterwards?"

"I was there on the night she won. When she came offstage, she gave me a hug, and I thought perhaps things between us could still be the same. I was just kidding myself. The press followed us around. Everyone wanted Starr; nobody cared who I was. After a while, I began to feel like I was an embarrassment to her, so I backed off and let her get on with it. I thought that maybe, after everything had calmed down, we'd get back together again. But she stopped calling, and she wouldn't take my calls."

"Did you talk about it with her? Decide to call it a day?"

"No. It just sort of ended."

"So, when was the last time you saw Carol?"

"Not for several weeks."

"Okay, Johnny. Thank you very much for your time."

I came away with the picture of a very sad young man. He'd obviously thought he'd found his life partner, but had lost her to 'celebrity'.

\*\*\*

The lady at FairyAid had given me the address of Billy Somemates, the goblin, who put together the houses for the starlight fairies. His workshop was in a small building close to Candlefield Park. And when I say *small*, I really do mean *small*. It was half the height of the surrounding buildings, and appeared to provide workshops specifically for the goblin community. I called at reception, where I was forced to crouch, otherwise I would have banged my head on the ceiling.

"Hello there," the female goblin behind the counter greeted me. "Are you okay? You look a bit uncomfortable."

"The ceiling is a little low for me."

"I'm sorry about that. When they constructed this building, they worked on the assumption that only goblins would use it. But, although the units are rented exclusively to goblins, there are lots of non-goblin customers. A stupid oversight, really. Who is it that you're here to see?"

"Billy Somemates?"

"Billy is in unit twenty-seven." She pointed at the corridor to her right.

By the time I reached Billy's unit, I had a crick in my neck.

"Are you okay?" The goblin looked up at me.

"I'm fine thanks. Are you Billy Somemates?"

"That's me."

"I'm Jill Gooder. I've just been with the people at FairyAid. I understand you build houses for the starlight fairies."

"I don't actually build them, but I do fit them out. The outside structure is bought ready-made; I just fit the interiors."

"That's pretty much what they told me. Could I come in and talk to you for a moment?"

"Of course, but do mind your head."

Once inside, I decided it was easier just to sit on the floor. At least that way, I could straighten my neck again. "Do I call you Mr Somemates?"

"No. Call me Billy, please."

"If you wouldn't mind, Billy, can you talk me through the process of putting together the houses?"

"Certainly. As I said, the exterior is bought ready-made with the windows and doors drawn onto the shell of the house. I turn them into fully functional windows and doors. I put in a floor to make it a two-level building, and then I put in dividers to create the individual rooms. Finally, I fit out the rooms with all the usual furnishings."

"That must be a very complicated procedure. They're so small."

"It is. Look, why don't I show you — it'll be easier. Come over here to my workbench."

I made my way over on all fours. There, on the workbench, were lots of little houses.

"I use this for the detailed work." He picked up one of the houses, and put it under an enormous magnifying glass. The tools he was using were similar to those I'd seen used to repair watches.

"So you see, Jill, I use these materials to create the building's interior. This one is partially done. I've opened up the windows and the door, and installed the floor. This one here is on the next stage — I've just put in the dividers to create the separate rooms. This one over here is ready to go out."

"Do you do all of this by yourself?"

"Yes, it's just me. It's a very skilled job as you might imagine. So far, I haven't been able to train anyone to help me. I wish I could find someone because the fairies are really desperate for these houses."

"It must help that you get the exterior shell ready-made."

"It most certainly does."

"I hope you don't mind me asking, but aren't those exteriors actually thimbles?"

"Yes, they are. All I have to do to the shell is to convert the doors and windows."

"Where do you buy the thimbles from?"

"There's only one place in Candlefield that has the right kind. That's The Finger. It's in the marketplace."

"How much do they cost you?"

"I can't remember offhand, but I think they're about three or four pounds each."

"Do you buy them in bulk?"

"No, usually just three or four at a time."

"I see. And do you personally go to The Finger to buy them?"

"No. I'm too busy putting together the houses. My assistant, Harlan, buys them for me."

"Is Harlan a goblin too?"

"No. Harlan is an elf."

"Is he here at the moment?"

"No, he only works part-time. He does bits and bobs around the place, and keeps things tidy. And, I let him buy the thimbles. It saves me wasting time going over there."

"Thank you very much for your time, Billy. It's been really helpful."

"Not at all. It's nice to have a visitor."

I crawled on hands and knees all the way out of the building.

Things were slowly starting to click into place. It was obvious that I needed to speak to Harlan.

*** 

While I was in Candlefield, I decided to pop into Cuppy C. After all of that crawling around on hands and knees, I needed a sit-down with a nice latte and a strawberry cupcake. Amber came to join me at the window table.

"I'm glad of a sit-down." I took a bite of cupcake. "I've been crawling around on my hands and knees for the last half-hour."

"Why? What have you been up to?"

Just then, Pearl joined us.

"I went to see the goblin who makes the houses for the starlight fairies."

"Mum told us about the housing shortage," Amber said. "It's terrible."

"Those little houses are so cute," Pearl said.

It was only then that I spotted the chairs stacked in the corner of the room. "What happened there?"

"The fire eater got a little carried away. They're scorched. It's a good thing no one was sitting at that particular table."

"Fire eater? Have you started hiring circus performers too?"

"No. Miles said we could share his."

"He did what?"

"He said they didn't need them all day, so we could have them after they'd finished at Best Cakes."

"How much is he going to charge you?"

"Nothing. He said he had to pay for them anyway, and thought it would be a nice gesture to make up for the rat incident."

"What's the catch?"

"That's what we're trying to work out. There has to be one."

I thought back to the last time I'd seen Miles. He'd been so desperate because of the situation with the Neverending Wool, he'd promised that if I talked Grandma around, he'd close down Best P.I. Services, and would stop the dirty tricks against Cuppy C and Ever A Wool Moment. I knew that Grandma had reversed the spell. Maybe Miles had turned over a new leaf. Or had he?

"How did the fire eater manage to scorch the chairs?"

"It was Pearl's fault." Amber got in quickly.

"No, it wasn't!" Pearl objected.

"You were the one who'd taken Barry for a walk."

"How was I supposed to know the fire-eater was allergic to dog hair? I only walked past him."

"Just as he was putting the fire in his mouth. You made him sneeze."

"Maybe you should have stuck with the origami?" I suggested. "By the way, how's it going with the guys? Have they forgiven you yet?"

"Yes, but *we* haven't forgiven *you*."

"Moi?" I put on my innocent face.

"Yes, you." Pearl grinned. "*The girls would love to go to all the BoundBall practices.*"

"Oh, yeah. I'd forgotten about that."

"Luckily for you, the guys decided they'd rather we weren't there. According to them, we moaned too much."

"Cheek!" Amber said. "We never moan."

# Chapter 11

I'd decided to finish early, and was on my way back to the flat when I got a phone call from Kathy. She sounded rather stressed.

"Jill, your grandmother has gone AWOL, and left me all by myself in the shop. I'm meant to be picking the kids up from school. Are you busy at the moment? Could you go and pick them up for me? Otherwise I'm going to have to close the shop."

I could have lied and pretended I was busy, but even I'm not that despicable. Well, not all the time, anyway.

"Yeah, okay. I'll make my way over there now. Do you know where Grandma has gone?"

"No. She never said a word. I thought she was in the back office, but when I went to tell her I was leaving, there was no sign of her. I've searched the shop and tea room, but she's nowhere to be seen. If you could pick up the kids, that would be great. Thanks."

I parked a couple of streets away from the school, and walked from there. There was a crossing patrol in front of the school gates, and as I got closer, I recognised the person wearing the white uniform, holding the yellow 'lollipop'.

"Daze?"

"Hi, Jill. What are you doing here?"

"I'm collecting my sister's kids. Grandma's done a disappearing act, so Kathy's having to look after the wool shop. More to the point, what are *you* doing here?"

"Undercover, as usual. We've had reports of a wicked witch turning kids into gingerbread men."

"Really? That's horrible."

"I know — we've issued a red alert."

"That sound serious."

"It's the highest state of alert. Blaze is over at the next school, and we've drafted in six more RRs to cover the other schools in this area. If she shows her ugly face, we'll can her sorry backside."

"That's reassuring. I'll go and collect the little darlings. Catch you later, Daze."

"Auntie Jill! Auntie Jill!" Lizzie threw her arms around me.

"Where's Mum?" Mikey shouted.

"She's had to work late in the shop, so I said I'd collect you."

"Can we go to the sweet shop, please, Auntie Jill?" Lizzie said.

I was wise to their tricks. They'd landed me in trouble before for buying them sweets. I wasn't about to be fooled again.

"Sorry, no. Mummy said I had to take you straight home today."

"Aw, Auntie Jill. Please." Lizzie pouted.

"No, I'm sorry. You got me in trouble last time. We've got to go straight home."

They were in full-on sulk mode when they climbed into the back seat of the car, but I ignored them, and drove straight to Kathy's.

"You haven't seen our slide, have you, Auntie Jill?" Lizzie seemed to have forgiven me by the time we reached their house.

"What slide? I didn't know you had one."

"Daddy bought us a slide and a swing. They're in the back garden. Would you like to see them?"

"Sure. After you've got changed."

On my way into the house, I noticed that the next door neighbours still had the chickens. I made the kids get changed first. I would have been in trouble if they'd got mud on their school clothes.

"Come on, Auntie Jill. Come on the slide." Lizzie dragged me around the back of the house.

Peter had put up a small slide and a swing in the back garden where the compost heap used to be.

"Would you like to go on the slide, Auntie Jill?"

"I don't think so. I'm a bit too big."

Mikey appeared. And so did his drum!

"I wouldn't play the drum out here. You'll scare the chickens."

"It doesn't scare them, Auntie Jill. They like to dance to it. Look!" He walked over to the fence, and began hammering away on the drum. The chickens started to run around in circles; no doubt trying to escape the awful noise.

"I'm not sure they're dancing, Mikey."

"They are! Look at that one. It's twirling around."

"Why don't I hold your drum while you go on the swing?"

"I don't like the swing. It's boring. I want to go on the slide."

The two of them took turns on the slide while I sat on the bench that was underneath the back window. I was almost asleep when a frantic voice made me stir.

I stood up, and went to see who was shouting, and where the fire was.

"Hello, can I help?"

"Is Kathy in?"

"No, I'm sorry. She's had to work late. I'm Jill, her sister."

"Oh dear." The woman looked distraught.

"Is there something I can help with?"

"I don't know what to do. My kids go to the same school as Mikey and Lizzie. They should have been home twenty minutes ago, but there's no sign of them. I've checked at the school, but they're not there. I'm worried something has happened to them."

"Have you contacted the police?"

"No. I suppose I should."

"Would you like to borrow my phone?"

It was too late. She'd already rushed across the road.

Daze's words echoed around my head: wicked witch, gingerbread men.

I gave her a ring. "Daze, it's Jill. Are you still on the school crossing patrol?"

"No, I've just finished."

"Okay. This may be nothing, but I've just had one of Kathy's friends come over here. Her two kids are usually home by now, but they haven't turned up. I just wondered—"

"The wicked witch?"

"Do you think it could be her?"

"It's possible. We've had a sighting of her halfway between this school and the one that Blaze is working at. If those kids walked home that way, then maybe."

"That doesn't sound good. If they've been turned into gingerbread, their poor mother will be devastated."

"It's okay, Blaze is tracking her as we speak. I'll catch up with him, and see if the kids are with her."

"Will you keep me posted?"

"Of course. I'll give you a call as soon as I have any news."

"Okay, thanks Daze."

Ten minutes later, Kathy's car pulled into the driveway.

"Are the kids all right?" She came rushing into the house.

"Of course they are."

"Where are they?"

"Around the back. They're playing on the slide."

"Are you sure?"

"Look, there they are."

She saw the kids and sighed with relief. "I was so worried."

"I know you think I'm hopeless at everything, but I can look after two kids for thirty minutes."

"It wasn't that. It's just that Sheila called me at work. Her two kids have gone missing."

"It must have been Sheila who came around here earlier. She was looking for you. Have they found them yet?"

"I don't think so. When she told me, I tried to call you, but you were engaged."

That must have been when I was talking to Daze.

"Sorry, Kathy. I didn't realise you'd called."

"I shut up shop, and came straight over. Your grandmother will just have to deal with it. It's not my fault if she goes AWOL."

I followed Kathy out to the garden where she gave Mikey and Lizzie a big hug.

"Poor Sheila," she said to me. "She must be distraught."

My phone rang. "Just a second, Kathy. I need to take this."

I went back into the house, so Kathy wouldn't overhear.

"Daze? What's happening?"

"Everything's okay, Jill. The wicked witch had the kids with her, but we got to her in time. She's locked up in Candlefield."

"What about the kids?"

"They're fine. We cast the 'forget' spell, and sent them on their way. They should be home any minute now."

"That's great. Thanks, Daze."

I went back outside. "The kids are okay, Kathy."

"How do you know?"

Whoops! That was a good question.

"I read it on my news app."

Kathy took out her phone. "There's nothing on mine about it."

"Let's go and check with your friend."

Kathy grabbed the kids, and we all started down the street.

"That's them!" Kathy pointed. "That's Sheila's kids!"

At that moment, Sheila came rushing out of her house, and hurried over to her kids.

"Thank goodness," Kathy said. "They're back safe."

"Yeah, thank goodness."

"I still don't understand how you knew, Jill."

"My app must be more up to date than yours."

\*\*\*

The next morning, I headed back to Middle Tweaking. Myrtle had set up two more interviews: The first with

Justin Flower, who was the baker in the village, and the other with Harry Payne, the butcher. As before, I met up with her at the old watermill.

"Jill, I know I told you nine o'clock, but I've just had a call from Justin Flower. He said he needs to put it back fifteen minutes. We may as well have a cup of tea while we're waiting."

"Okay, that would be great."

"Custard creams?"

"Absolutely. Thanks."

The more I got to know Myrtle, the more I liked the old girl. When she'd first walked into my office, I'd made the mistake of stereotyping her. I'd thought she was just an old biddy who probably spent all of her time knitting and baking. In fact, nothing could have been further from the truth. Myrtle was so switched on, it wasn't true. It took me all my time just to keep up with her. She had all the latest gadgets: tablet, smartphone, you name it, she'd got it. She knew her way around the internet far better than I did. Myrtle struck me as a tough old bird. She was certainly nobody's fool.

"Tell me, Myrtle. How did you end up living here in Middle Tweaking?"

"I was born here."

"Have you lived all your life here?"

"No. I moved away for many years after university."

"Doing what? What was your job?"

"I can't tell you that."

"I bet it was exciting. Did you come back to Middle Tweaking after you'd retired?"

"Retired?" She recoiled. "I don't like that word. There are some people who believe you have a sell-by date. It doesn't seem to matter to them how capable or physically fit you are. You reach a certain number, and that's it—you're done. Goodbye. Here's your pension."

"Is that what happened to you?"

"More or less, but I'm not ready for retirement. I doubt I ever will be. I like to keep active. That's one of the reasons I get involved with these investigations." She glanced at her watch. "Come on. It's time to pay a visit to Justin."

Either Justin Flower was wearing three-week old socks, or something had curled up and died in his front room. I kept glancing at Myrtle to see if she'd noticed, but she didn't seem to. Maybe she had trouble with her sinuses.

"Who's this?" He glared at me.

"I did tell you, Justin," Myrtle said, as cool, calm and collected as always. "This is Jill Gooder. She was at the final murder mystery evening, and is helping with my investigation."

"I don't see why you need to investigate at all, Myrtle. You're not the police."

"Is there some reason you don't want to talk to me, Justin?" Her eyes burned into him. "Do you have something to hide?"

"No. Of course not."

"Then what possible harm can it do for us to have a chat? We are neighbours, after all."

Myrtle was quick to take command of the situation. I was impressed.

"So, Justin," she said. "How did you get on with Madge?"

"I didn't like her."

"That's honest, at least. And why was that?"

"She almost put me out of business."

"How did she do that?"

"She reported me to Trading Standards. She said she'd found a dead fly in one of my cakes."

"Had she?"

"Of course not. There are no flies or any other insects in my bakery. It's spotless. There must have been a dead fly on the worktop when she cut the cake. The whole thing was ridiculous. She didn't even have the courtesy to come and tell me first; she just reported it to Trading Standards. They came to see me, and carried out an inspection of the bakery. You know what those people are like. They're vicious jobsworths. They insisted I make all kinds of unnecessary improvements. It cost me a small fortune."

"Are you sure that it was Madge who reported you?"

"Of course I am. Who else would it have been? She was always tutting about the cleanliness of the shop."

"Did you actually ask her if she was the one?"

"Of course. She had the audacity to come into the shop after the inspector had been. I refused to serve her. When she asked why, I said it was because she'd reported me to Trading Standards."

"What did she say to that?"

"She didn't deny it. She just turned around and walked out."

"What about the affair with the lottery?"

"That's another thing. She cheated us all out of our money."

"You don't think she might have forgotten on that one occasion?"

"Of course not. She knew the odds of us winning were so small that instead of putting the bet on, she pocketed the money. I reckon she'd been doing it for months. She must have made a small fortune off us. Then when our numbers came up, she was in a right pickle. That's why she pretended she'd forgotten."

"Some of the other players believed her. I take it you didn't?"

"Not for one moment."

"Okay, thank you for being so candid, Justin."

# Chapter 12

Our next appointment was with Harry Payne. When Myrtle knocked on his door, it was a woman who answered—a woman with shocking red hair.

"Hello, Barbara," Myrtle said. "Harry is expecting us."

"Not here, he isn't."

"He told me ten o' clock."

"That's as maybe, but Harry doesn't live here anymore."

"Since when?"

"Since when is it any of your business?"

Myrtle didn't respond. Instead, she engaged her secret weapon—a kind of death-ray glare.

"If you must know, since two weeks ago. I threw him out. I'm surprised you haven't heard."

"I had no idea. I bumped into him in the village, and arranged to meet him at ten. He never mentioned he'd moved out."

"He probably assumed you'd heard. There's been a lot of gossip."

"Where's he staying?"

"Where do you think? His second home: The Old Trout."

"Look, this is none of my business, Barbara, but—"

"That's never stopped you before, Myrtle."

"I was just wondering why you threw him out?"

"Why do you think? He's been up to his old tricks again."

Myrtle nodded. It was amazing how quickly she could transform from interrogator to Agony Aunt.

"I thought he'd grown out of it." Barbara continued. "A

few years ago, he regularly went off with some pretty, young thing, but he always came back. But then, I put my foot down and told him enough was enough. I told him straight that if he ever did it again, that would be the end for him and me."

"I'm really sorry." Myrtle took Barbara's hand in hers. "You deserve better."

"You're right, I do. What did you want to see Harry about, anyway?"

"We wanted a quick word about Madge."

"Of course. I should have guessed. I doubt he'll have a good word to say about her. It was because of Madge that I discovered he was cheating again."

"How did that happen exactly?"

Myrtle had Barbara eating out of her hand now.

"He thought he was being clever. He'd got himself a P.O. box at the post office. He'd been using it for any correspondence which he didn't want me to see. Anyway, a couple of weeks ago, a letter dropped onto the doormat. It was addressed to Harry, c/o the P.O. box number. That shouldn't have happened. Harry had set it up, so that the mail remained at the post office until he collected it. It was two tickets for Bravo, a West End show. I'd been trying to get Harry to take me to see it for months, but he said it was too expensive. At first, I thought he'd bought the tickets as a surprise for me, but then I saw the names printed on them. One was his, but the other wasn't mine. It was one of his young assistants."

When Barbara took a deep breath to compose herself, Myrtle gave her hand a reassuring squeeze.

"So, I packed his bags, and threw them in the front garden."

"Good for you, Barbara. How did he take it?"

"He was more annoyed than upset."

"Annoyed with you? He had a cheek."

"Not with me. With Madge, for letting the letter slip through. He tried grovelling his way back in, but I wasn't having any of it."

"You did the right thing, Barbara. Thanks for your help."

After leaving Barbara, Myrtle and I made our way to The Old Trout.

"How do you do that?" I said.

"Do what?"

"Be *good cop, bad cop* all in one?"

"I didn't realise that's what I was doing."

"One minute you had her scared to death. The next, you were her best friend."

"What's your approach, Jill?"

"I tend to jump in feet first. Speak first, and think later. I'm more *bad cop, horrible cop*."

That brought a smile to Myrtle's face. "Living out here in the countryside probably makes a difference. I'm not sure your approach would go down well here. Anyway, what did you make of what Barbara had to say?"

"I don't imagine Harry Payne was very happy with Madge Hick after that letter slipped through."

"What makes you think it *slipped* through?"

"Do you think it might have been deliberate?"

"I don't know. I'm just playing devil's advocate."

"Either way, he wouldn't have been very happy about it, but it's hardly a motive for murder."

We caught up with Harry Payne in one of the rooms above The Old Trout.

"You didn't mention you were living here, Harry," Myrtle scolded him.

"Sorry. My head's all over the place."

He didn't look like he'd had a shave for at least a couple of days. His hair was dishevelled, and his clothes looked like he'd slept in them. All in all, he looked a bit of a shambles.

"I've just spoken to Barbara," Myrtle said.

"Is she still angry with me?"

"What do you think?"

"It's all Madge's fault."

Myrtle engaged the death-ray glare again. "You don't think you might have been partly to blame?"

"Well, yeah." He back-pedalled. "Obviously, I shouldn't have bought the tickets."

"Or been seeing another woman?"

"Or that. But, if Madge had kept the letter at the post office like she was supposed to, none of this would have happened."

Myrtle rolled her eyes. Harry Payne was three steps beyond stupid.

"Did you have it out with Madge?"

"Of course I did, but she claimed it was a mistake. Just like she did with the lottery. Very convenient mistake if you ask me. I pay over a hundred pounds a year for that post office box. I expected her to do her job right for that kind of money. Instead, she gets me thrown out of my house. I'm running out of clothes."

If he was expecting sympathy from me or Myrtle, he was going to be very disappointed.

"Anyway, it's finished between me and Rosie now. She's gone and got herself a job at the abattoir. Do you think Barbara would take me back if I told her that?"

"I'm sure she would," Myrtle said. "You should go around there after we've left."

"Yeah, I think I will. I hate it here. This room smells like old frogs."

After we'd left, I walked back to my car with Myrtle.

"Do you really think Barbara will take him back?"

"Of course not. She'll probably kick his backside all around the village."

"You crafty old thing. I like it."

"Not so much of the 'old', thank you." She grinned. "Let's have a quick recap. So far we have Harry Payne who had a grudge against Madge because, in his eyes, she'd got him thrown out of the matrimonial home. And then there's Justin Flower, who believed that Madge had reported him to Trading Standards. Florence Long seems an unlikely candidate, but does have access to the pharmacy. And we still have Brendan Breeze to interview. Any thoughts so far, Jill?"

"None of those we've interviewed strikes me as a murderer, but I've been wrong before. I'd really like to get inside Madge's house, and take a look around. Do you think that's going to be possible?"

"Through official channels? Probably not. But I might be able to arrange it—leave it to me; I'll talk to oddjobs."

Oddjobs? Before I could ask, she'd turned and walked away.

***

Mrs V was at her desk; sitting next to her, with his hands covered in wool, was none other than Armi.

"Hi, Armi. You're becoming a regular visitor."

He could barely meet my gaze. "Hello, Jill."

"I see Mrs V has got you helping with the wool again."

"Annabel says I have the hands for it." He laughed nervously.

It looked as though reversing the spell had done the trick. Armi was back to his old self.

"By the way, Jill," he said. "I want to apologise for anything I may have said or done over the last forty-eight hours."

"What do you mean?"

"I don't know what came over me, but I haven't been myself for a couple of days. I became rather loud and obnoxious. I know I upset Annabel a little."

"Yes, but you're forgiven now." Mrs V patted his shoulder.

"I've upset Gordon too. He's barely talking to me."

"I shouldn't worry about that." I grinned. "It's probably no bad thing to stand up to Gordon every now and again. He can be awfully overbearing."

"You may be right, but it's not something I'm used to doing. I've always admired how you stand up to him. Anyway, if I did say anything inappropriate, I apologise. I don't know what came over me."

"Are you taking any meds, Armi?"

"Just something for my sinuses."

"That might be it. Look at what happened to me the other day. I came over very peculiar after I'd taken those hay fever meds. I even called you a goblin."

"I'm never likely to forget that. Maybe I should talk to the pharmacist about changing brands."

Winky was in the windowsill. His tiny flags had been discarded, and in their place, he was holding a remote control. Moments later, a small helicopter came through the window. He grabbed it, tore off the note and read it. Then he scribbled a reply, which he attached before sending the chopper on its way. It was just like old times.

Winky's last remote control helicopter had crashed and burned.

"Where did you get the new helicopter from?"

"I ordered it online. It came this morning."

"With my credit card, I assume?"

"Of course."

"I hope it didn't cost too much."

"What price love?"

"Why didn't you get Bonnie and Clive to pay?"

"Who?"

"Bella's owners—err—I mean the people Bella lives with."

"They're humans. They wouldn't understand."

"So muggins here has to foot the bill again?"

"What are you complaining about? I hear you have a paying case for a change."

"I do actually. And it involves a well-known TV celebrity."

"Starr Fish?" He laughed. "Do me a favour. She was Z-list at best. Unlike me."

"You? Since when are you a celebrity?"

"A-list regular, that's me."

"I've never seen you in the gossip pages."

"That's because you don't read the feline mags: Whiskers, Fur and Claws. I'm always in one of them. Bella too."

"If you're such a big time celebrity, how come you don't pay your way?"

"That's what *you* are for."

Nice to know.


Twenty minutes later, Winky had said his goodbyes, via helicopter, to Bella, and he was curled up asleep on the sofa.

The room suddenly went a little chilly. A moment later, Colonel Briggs' ghost appeared. I was surprised to see he was by himself. Something was obviously amiss.

"Colonel, are you okay?"

"Not really, Jill."

"Whatever's the matter? Is it Priscilla?"

"Sort of, yes."

"She's not ill, is she?"

"She's a ghost, Jill. She's dead — she can't get much more ill than that."

"Of course, sorry. I keep forgetting about that. What is it, then?"

"You know we moved back to the house?"

"Yes. How are things working out up there?"

"Everything was fine. Until Matthew turned up."

"Who's he?"

"A ghost. Matthew Most."

Matthew Most the ghost? "Where did he come from?"

"That's a jolly good question. I'd always understood that ghosts could only haunt buildings where they'd lived during their lifetime, or a building occupied by a relative or close friend. It seems this guy moves in anywhere that takes his fancy. He first turned up three or four days ago. Since then, he's made a real nuisance of himself. What's worse, he's obviously taken with Cilla; he's been flirting outrageously with her."

"How does Priscilla feel about that?"

"I have to be honest, Jill. I'm a little disappointed in her. I thought we had a good thing going, but Matthew seems to have turned her head. She denies it, but I've seen the look in her eye when he's around."

"Are you both still wandering around in the nude?"

"Not since he showed up. It just doesn't feel right."

"I thought you two had really hit it off."

"Me too. The reason I popped in to see you is because I seem to recall you have a friend who is a Ghost Hunter?"

"Yes. Mad Lane. She helped me with Battery."

"That's what I thought. I wondered if she might be able to do a little sniffing around to see if she could find out anything about Mr Matthew Most. There's something about him that feels a little shady. Could you ask your friend to see if she can turn up anything?"

"No problem. I'll have a word with her."

"Thanks, Jill. You're a good friend."

\*\*\*

It was time to talk to Harlan the elf. I'd got his address from Billy Somemates. Harlan lived very close to Candlefield swimming baths—somewhere I hadn't yet got around to visiting. I hadn't told Billy of my suspicions because I thought it only fair to talk to Harlan first.

When I knocked on the tiny door, a little elf in a very

pleasing green hat, popped his head out. "Hello, can I help you?" he squeaked.

"Are you Harlan?"

"Yes, who are you? If you're selling, you're wasting your time. I never buy at the door."

"I'm not selling anything."

"Are you sure? That's what the man who sold me the chimney brush said."

"Your house doesn't have a chimney."

"I know. He was very persuasive."

"I promise I'm not here to sell you anything. My name is Jill Gooder. I've been talking to the people at FairyAid, and also to Billy Somemates."

"I see."

"Billy told me you work part-time for him."

"That's right."

"Look, I'll get straight to the point. I understand that you're responsible for buying the thimbles from The Finger."

His face fell, and I knew I'd struck a chord. "Yes I am. What of it?"

"I was told by Tuppence Farthing, the owner of The Finger, that several house-themed thimbles have been stolen from her shop over the past few weeks. And yet, Billy told me that he gives you the money to buy them."

"Oh dear. You're perfectly right. I've been taking them."

"But why would you do that?"

"I didn't keep the money for myself. I thought if I didn't have to pay for the thimbles that I'd be able to donate it back to FairyAid, and they'd be able to build even more houses."

"Are you telling me that you've been stealing the

thimbles, and then donating the money, which should have been used to buy them, to FairyAid?"

"That's right. I shouldn't have done that, should I?"

"Definitely not. Look, I'm sorry, but I have no choice but to tell Tuppence Farthing what's been going on. It might help if you were to come with me. Would you be willing to do that?"

"Yes." He sighed. "I suppose I'd better."

We walked together to The Finger. Tuppence Farthing was behind the counter; she greeted me with a warm smile.

"Hi, Jill."

"There's someone here who'd like a few words with you, Tuppence."

Only then did she notice Harlan who barely came up to my calf.

"This is Harlan."

"Pleased to meet you, Harlan."

He jumped up onto the counter, so they were face to face. "I—err—I have a confession to make. I was tasked with buying thimbles for Billy Somemates who makes the houses for the starlight fairies. But, instead of buying them I sneaked into your shop, and took them without paying."

Tuppence looked shocked. "Why would you do that?"

"I realise it's no excuse, but I wanted as many houses as possible for the fairies, so I gave the money back to FairyAid. I'm very sorry, and I'll understand if you want to call the police. I'll be happy to make a full confession."

"There's no need to involve the police. I just wish you'd spoken to me. I had no idea that's what the thimbles were being used for. How about from now on, I sell you the thimbles at cost price? When you need the next batch, come and see me, and I'll make sure you get the best deal. You'll get twice as many as you would if you were buying them at full price. How does that sound?"

"Thank you. That's so very generous," Harlan said. "And of course, I'll pay you back for those that I've already taken."

"No need. Call those my donation to Fairy Aid."

"Thank you so much." Harlan was obviously touched by Tuppence's kindness.

"And thank you for getting to the bottom of this, Jill." Tuppence said. "It never occurred to me that it would be something like this."

"My pleasure. I'm just pleased this means that the fairies will get more houses."

# Chapter 13

The next person on my list to interview, in connection with the Starr Fish case, was her new boyfriend—a guy who went by the name of Scott Venus. Call it intuition if you like, but something told me that wasn't his real name. Like Starr Fish, he'd probably decided that his real name wasn't showbiz enough, so he'd changed it to something completely and utterly ludicrous.

Scott lived in what was known locally as the Glass Tower. It was the largest of three apartment blocks built three years ago in the centre of Washbridge. They were ultra-expensive—way above my pay grade. It was my first time inside the building; it was gorgeous. Why didn't I live somewhere like that? It probably had something to do with my lack of work. And money. Maybe I should have considered going on a reality TV show. If Kathy could do it, surely I could. I quite liked the idea of having people chase after me for autographs. Maybe I could charge for those too. Jack and I would be on the front page of all those celebrity magazines.

What? Who are you calling Walter?

Scott Venus lived in apartment two-one-seven.

"Who are you?" He didn't look much like a Scott. More a Fred or an Arthur.

"My name's Jill Gooder. I'm a private investigator."

"What do you want?"

Nice to know his Z-list celebrity status hadn't affected his good manners.

"I'd like a few words about Starr Fish."

"What about her?"

"Do you think we could go inside rather than talk out

here where everyone can hear us."

"I suppose so." He huffed.

The furnishings were high quality, and matched the building itself, but the place was a dump. There was 'stuff' everywhere. What was it with men? Did *any* of them have the 'tidy' gene?

"What do you want to know?" He took a bite of what looked like yesterday's pizza. "Want some?" He offered me the box.

"No, thanks." I'm good for salmonella.

"I believe you and Starr were an item?"

"Not really." A small piece of pizza fell onto the carpet. At least the mice wouldn't go hungry.

"I thought you lived together?"

"Yeah, but we had separate rooms."

"So you weren't in a relationship with Starr?"

"Nah." He took a slug from a huge bottle of flat Coke. "That was just for publicity."

"How do you mean?"

"Our manager said the tabloids would pay more attention to a reality TV 'couple'. He reckoned they'd be falling over themselves to run stories on us."

"How did that work out?"

"It didn't. They only cared about Starr. When we were together they were only ever interested in her. I might as well have been invisible."

"How did you feel about that?"

"How do you think? I wasn't happy about it. I was trying to raise my profile, so I could get more money for doing personal appearances, and to help sell more copies of my book."

"What book?"

"My autobiography, of course."

"Of course. Have you already written it?"

"*I'm* not writing it. Some toast-writer is doing that."

"Ghost."

"What?

"It's a *ghost*-writer not a *toast*-writer."

"Oh? That makes more sense. I never did get the whole toast thing."

Wow! Just wow!

"Did you and Starr argue a lot?"

"Not all that much, but then I didn't really see much of her. She was always going down to London to do an interview or to have her photograph taken. I think she was planning to move down there."

"Did you go out as a couple?"

"We went to parties and premieres, and stuff like that together, but it was only for the cameras; we didn't have anything in common."

"It must have made you angry that she was getting all the attention?"

"Of course it did." He hesitated between mouthfuls of pizza. "Hang on, though. That doesn't mean I wanted to hurt her if that's what you're thinking. I could never do something like that. My mum would kill me."

I came away with the impression that Scott was obviously jealous and frustrated that Starr had attracted much more media attention than he'd managed. Even so, I couldn't convince myself that he had it in him to kill her. Underneath his celebrity 'front', Scott Venus was still a 'mummy's boy'.

Back in the office, I searched online for images of the

'celebrity' couple. The majority of photos focussed more on Starr than on Scott. It was quite obvious that there was no magic or sparkle between them; they looked like two strangers standing next to one another. But it was something else which caught my eye. There was another familiar face, in the background in several of the photos. It was Starr's ex-boyfriend, Johnny Badger. When I'd spoken to him he'd told me that he'd moved on, and was no longer interested in Starr, but these photos appeared to tell a different story.

***

Mrs V came through to my office.

"What's *he* up to now?" She gestured to Winky who had just finished sending semaphore messages to Bella.

"He's looking out of the window."

"I don't trust him."

Winky turned around, and gave her a one-eyed glare.

"See the way he looks at me? It's like he hates me."

"She's got that much right," Winky said under his breath.

"I'm sure that's not true. It's that eye of his which makes him look mean."

Mrs V looked unconvinced — with good reason.

"Was there something you wanted, Mrs V?"

"Oh yes. I almost forgot. That friend of yours is out front. The librarian."

"Mad? Send her in, would you?"

"It's none of my business." Mrs V lowered her voice to a whisper. "But I think she's let herself go a little. Maybe you should have a word?"

"How do you mean, *'let herself go'*?"

"You'll see."

Mrs V showed Mad in, and then left us alone.

"Hey, Jill." Mad seemed bright enough.

"Grab a seat. You've got Mrs V a little worried."

"Me? Why?"

"She thinks you're letting yourself go."

"That's nice." Mad grinned. "It must be the hair."

Normally when Mad was at work, she wore her hair in a bun, but today she'd let it down.

"It does look a little wild."

"I know. That bun drives me crazy. It makes my head itch like I've got lice. Come to think of it, now that Nails has moved in with Mum, I might have."

"Don't." I suddenly felt the urge to scratch my head.

"Tell Mrs V she doesn't have to worry about me. It'll be in a bun again when I go back to work after my lunch hour and a half."

"You get an hour and a half?"

"Officially no, but no one seems to notice."

"How's the ghost hunting going?"

"It's a bit quiet at the moment. I need some excitement. Maybe we should have another night out?"

"No chance. I haven't recovered from the last one yet. But I do have something which might ease the boredom for you."

"What's that?"

"Do you remember that friend of mine, the colonel?"

"Of course I do. Didn't he tip you off about that ugly thug who wanted to kill you? What was his name again? Carburettor?"

"Battery. Yeah, that was the colonel. He came to see me

the other day because he has a bit of a problem. He's recently moved back into his old house; the one he lived in before he died. He's living there with his new girlfriend, Priscilla. It seems that everything was going okay until another ghost turned up out of the blue. According to the colonel, this new ghost has no connection to the house. He just seems to be squatting there. What's even worse is that he's coming on to Priscilla. As you might imagine, the colonel is none too happy about any of this."

"This squatter—are you saying he didn't live in that house when he was alive? And has no relatives there?"

"That's right."

"And he wasn't invited by the colonel?"

"Definitely not."

"In that case, he's basically trespassing. There are strict rules which determine where a ghost can live—in other words, where he can haunt. He can try to attach himself to anyone, but unless he was known to that person, the connection is unlikely to succeed. Do you happen to know the ghost's name?"

"It's Matthew Most."

"Okay, I'll look into it, and let you know what I find out."

"Thanks, Mad, you're a good friend."

"Hmm? Let's see if you still think so in a couple of minutes' time."

Oh dear, I didn't like the sound of that one little bit.

"What do you mean?"

"The reason I'm here is to invite you over for dinner."

"At your place?"

"Yeah. My mother said that she wanted to show her

gratitude for the way you helped me when I was charged with Anita Pick's murder."

"There's really no need. You're a friend. I was glad I could help."

"That's what I told her, but she insists that you come over for a meal at our place."

"When?"

"I'm not sure, but I'll let you know."

"Okay, I'll be there."

What had I just let myself in for?

\*\*\*

I'd been trying for ages to secure an interview with Starr Fish's manager—a man named Charlie Taylor, or apparently, Chaz to his friends. Whether he'd been avoiding me or had genuinely been busy, I had no way of knowing. Eventually though, my persistence paid off, and he agreed to meet me at his offices.

"Hello," the fresh faced young man behind reception said.

"Hi."

"How can I help you?"

"I'm here to see Mr Charlie Taylor."

"You mean Chaz. And who are you?"

"My name's Jill Gooder. I'm—"

"Oh, yes. Gooder. Chaz is expecting you. You can go through now. It's that door on the right."

"Thanks."

Chaz Taylor should have been prosecuted for his taste in shirts: Dolphins, lighthouses and mermaids? A blue cravat was the finishing touch.

"I don't have long," he greeted me.

Obviously not long enough to give due consideration to his wardrobe.

"That's all right, Mr Taylor. I know you're a busy man. I like your shirt."

"Thanks. It's one of my favourites. Call me Chaz. Everybody calls me Chaz."

Flattery did it every time.

"Okay Chaz. This shouldn't take very long. I wanted to ask you a few questions about Starr Fish."

"How come you're involved? Aren't the police handling this?"

"Yes, of course, but I often work alongside them." Whether they know it or not.

"I thought at one point they were going to arrest me."

"Why would they do that?"

"I was one of the last people to see Starr alive."

"What can you tell me about that meeting?"

"There's not much to tell. Starr was her usual obnoxious self. We ended up in a shouting match. She told me to butt out of her business, and her life."

"But weren't you her manager?"

"In theory, yes. In practice, debatable."

"How do you mean?"

"I made it my business to sign up the contestants who were going into Life at the Top before the show started."

"Did they *all* sign up?"

"Of course they did. They couldn't wait to be famous."

"What went wrong between you and Starr?"

"The stroppy little cow accused me of trying to rip her off."

"In what way?"

"You would have to ask her."

"I can hardly do that now, can I. You must know why she wasn't happy?"

"Someone turned her head."

"What do you mean, 'turned her head'?"

"I mean what I say. Joey told her that I was ripping her off, and that the contract wasn't even legal. He promised her the earth if she'd sign with him."

"Who's Joey?"

"Joey Buttons. He's the bane of my life. He's a manager too, but he wants it handed to him on a plate. Instead of finding new stars, and nurturing them like I do, he waits until they've already made the headlines, then jumps in and tries to steal them away."

"And that's what happened with Starr?"

"Yes, as soon as she won the competition, and began to make all the headlines, Joey turned up."

"But, surely she was under contract to you."

"Of course she was, but that doesn't count for much these days. Those fancy lawyers can get almost any contract declared null and void. Joey knew I didn't have deep enough pockets to fight it in court, even if I did think I'd win."

"So, I guess your relationship with Starr was difficult."

"Impossible. She hated the idea of me getting any commission. In fact, she'd actually been arranging some of her own gigs recently."

# Chapter 14

The next morning, as I was just about to have breakfast, I realised I was out of coffee. What was I supposed to do now? I could nip across to the shops or —

"Morning, Kathy."

"Jill? What's wrong?"

"Nothing. I just thought I'd call to say good morning to my favourite sister."

"I'm busy. I have to get the kids ready for school."

Always with the excuses.

"I thought I'd pop over, if that's okay."

"Right now?"

"Yeah. Have a coffee ready for me, would you? And a slice of toast would be nice."

I ended the call before she could object.

What? Can I help it if I love my sister so much?

Before I got to the car, my phone rang. I assumed it would be Kathy, but it was Jack.

"Morning, pet—" He caught himself. "Jill."

"You nearly said it again, didn't you?"

"Said what?"

"You know what: petal."

"I wouldn't dare."

"You'd better not."

"I thought I'd better give you a call while I had a minute. I've been at the station since the crack of dawn. Things have been pretty hectic here, so I'm not sure when I'll be able to see you. It might be a few days."

"That's okay. Are you working on anything in particular?"

"Mainly the Starr Fish murder. As you can imagine, the

tabloids are having a field day with it."

"Are you making any progress?"

"Old habits die hard with you, don't they, Jill? Please tell me you haven't gone and got yourself involved with this case."

"Of course not. I was only asking out of interest."

"We haven't made much progress yet. There are a couple of odd things about this case, but nothing worth talking about."

"Go on. You can tell me. You know I'm always interested in murder cases."

"The really curious thing is that although the autopsy showed that Starr Fish was drowned, she wasn't drowned at Bar Fish."

"How can you possibly know that?"

"According to the experts, the water found in her lungs was not the same water as that in the tanks at Bar Fish. I don't really understand it, but they're certain she was drowned somewhere else, transported to Bar Fish, and placed in the tanks there."

"And, you don't have any leads so far?"

"Not a thing. Look, Jill, I've got to go—I've got a briefing in a few minutes. I'll catch up with you as soon as I can."

"Bye, Jack."


"I take it you've run out of coffee again." Kathy was really pleased to see me; she was just hiding it well.

"I'm not just here for your coffee."

"Don't come that. I can read you like a book."

"So, where is it?"

"On the kitchen table."

"What about my toast?"

"You know where the toaster is."

"Charming. Where's Peter?"

"You've just missed him. He's taken the kids to school."

"Are they okay?"

"They're both fine. Lizzie's next talent competition is soon. You'll be coming, won't you?"

"Of course." Wild horses couldn't drag me there.

"How's Jack? Have you seen anything of him recently?"

"He's busy on that reality TV star's murder, Starr Fish."

"Has he made any progress?"

"Not much. The problem is I'm working on it too."

"How come?"

"The owner of Bar Fish, Stuart Steele, came to see me."

"What does Jack think of that?"

"There's the thing."

"Don't tell me you haven't told him."

"Not exactly."

"By 'not exactly' I assume you mean 'not at all'? Have you spoken to him?"

"Yeah. Just now before I came over here."

"Did he mention the case?"

"Only when I asked him about it."

"Jill! Please tell me you weren't pumping him for information."

"'Pumping him for information' is a bit strong."

"I doubt he'll think it's a bit strong when he finds out. You're such an idiot, Jill. You've got a good thing going with Jack, and you're jeopardising it by lying to him."

"Anyhow, how's Peter." It was time to change the subject.

"He's great."

"Business all right?"

"The business is doing really well. He's landed lots of new customers, and he's been working all hours. I hardly see him."

"How do you both feel about that?"

"We're pleased to have the money, and thrilled that the business is doing well, but I'm not happy he's out of the house so much. But it should be okay now."

"How come?"

"Pete had mentioned to a few people that he was looking for someone to help him. An old colleague of his suggested someone. This guy has plenty of experience in the gardening business, and he's recently been made redundant, so Pete has taken him on a trial basis. So far, Pete's really pleased with him."

"That sounds promising." I finished the last of my coffee. "Anyway, I only popped over to make sure you were all okay."

"Not for the coffee, then?"

"You really have a low opinion of me, don't you?"

"Not as low as Jack will have when he finds out that you've been lying to him."

*\*\*\**

I'd parked the car, and was walking towards the office, when my phone rang.

"Jill, it's Stuart Steele."

"Hi."

"Would it be possible for us to meet up later today, at Bar Fish, for a quick drink and a catch up?"

"I suppose so, but to be honest, I don't really have

anything to tell you at the moment. It's early days."

"Even so, if we could meet for five or ten minutes, it might be useful. How does midday sound?"

"Sure, okay. I'll see you then."

When I got to the office, there was a note on Mrs V's desk which read: *Next door with Armi. Back in 15 minutes. Annabel.*

It seemed, my highly paid PA/receptionist had absconded in order to meet up with her boyfriend next door at Armitage, Armitage, Armitage, and Poole. I'd have to have words. I was just about to open the door to my office when I noticed another note attached to it: *World record attempt. Do not enter!*

How dare he? If Winky thought he could lock me out of my own office, he had another think coming. Stuff him!

My office was full of cats: one with a clipboard, another with a stopwatch, a third with a notebook, and one with a camera. They were all standing around Winky.

"Didn't you see the note?" Winky yelled at me.

"The one that said I couldn't come into my own office? Yeah, I saw it."

"And?"

"And, I ignored it."

"Lucky for you we haven't started yet."

"Haven't started *what* yet? Who are all these cats?"

"I'm trying to break the Meow World Record for juggling five balls. This gentleman is Marmaduke Masters. He's responsible for the circus skills section of the Meow World Records publication."

Marmaduke looked at me over his jam-jar lens glasses. "If you intend to stay in here, I must ask you to sit over there." He pointed to the sofa. "Take a seat and remain absolutely silent. It's essential for Mr Winky —"

"It's just Winky," Winky corrected him.

"It's essential that Winky is not distracted during the course of his world record attempt."

"Do as Marmaduke says." Winky gestured to the sofa.

Something wasn't quite right here. Why was I being ordered around in *my* office by a bunch of cats?

"Hurry up, please." Marmaduke ushered me along.

"Okay. How long will this take?"

"If he's to beat the current record, it must be at least thirty-six minutes and twenty-two seconds."

"You want me to sit there for thirty-six minutes?"

"And twenty-two seconds. Unless of course he was to drop one of the balls, in which case the attempt will have failed. Now, if you'll please sit down, I'd like to get this thing started."

It was pointless arguing with this crowd, so I took a seat on the sofa.

"Right, Winky," Marmaduke said. "I'm going to count you in. Are you ready?"

Winky nodded.

"Three, two, one, go."

Marmaduke's assistant pressed the button on his stopwatch, and Winky began to juggle the five balls. Even though I was annoyed about being ordered around in my own office, I couldn't help but admire Winky's skill. He kept those five balls up in the air with consummate ease; his level of concentration was incredible. I daren't move in case the sofa squeaked. If I was responsible for him failing in his world record attempt, I'd never hear the end of it.

Thirty minutes in, and he was getting close to the

record. I wanted to cheer him on, but thought it would probably put him off, so I remained silent.

Thirty-six minutes. Another twenty-two seconds, and he would have broken the record. Marmaduke glanced down at his colleague's stopwatch; I was watching the second hand on mine. Ten, nine, eight, seven, six, five, four, three, two, one.

He'd done it! I was just about to jump off the sofa and cheer, but realised he was going to carry on to set a new record. Seven minutes later, and he was still at it, but then, one of the balls fell to the ground. He'd beaten the record by a good seven minutes. There was a round of applause from the cats in the room, and Winky took a bow.

"Well done, Winky," Marmaduke said. "That's definitely a new record. You'll be in the next edition of Meow World Records, unless of course someone else beats it in the meantime."

Marmaduke and his assistant shook Winky's paw, but I noticed that the other two cats were headed towards me.

"Hello, gorgeous," the cat with the notepad said. "I believe Winky lives in this office with you."

"That's right, who are you?"

"Rory Dale. I'm a reporter for Claw Magazine. You've probably heard of it."

"I think Winky may have mentioned it."

"This juggling stuff is all very interesting, but what I'm really after is a story that our readers can get their claws into. I heard on the grapevine that Winky is currently dating an ex-catwalk model, Bella. Is that correct?"

"Yes, he is. He and Bella have been seeing one another for a while." I saw no reason to deny it. It wasn't like it was a secret.

"I see." The cat scribbled something in his notepad. "Am I right in thinking that recently Winky's brother, Socks, came to visit?"

"That's right." I didn't like where this was heading.

"And, would I be right in saying Bella and Socks had a fling?"

"I wouldn't know anything about that."

"Come now. The feline public has a right to know. If you were able to confirm the rumour, I might be able to run to a small fee."

"I think you should get out of here, right now!"

What was it with the press? Human or feline, they were all the same. If Rory Clawy thought he could get me to dish the dirt on Winky, he had another think coming.

Thirty minutes later, the officials from Meow World Records, and the reporters from Claw Magazine had all left. Winky was having a rest on the sofa, and looking very pleased with himself.

Mrs V was back.

"What's been going on in your office, Jill?" she said.

"Nothing. Why?"

"There seemed to be a lot of activity in there when I got back from seeing Armi."

"Just business as usual."

She obviously wasn't convinced, but I could hardly tell her the truth.

"Look, I have to nip out. I've arranged to meet with Stuart Steele."

"What shall I say if that nice young man of yours calls?"

"Jack? He won't. But if he does, don't tell him where I am. Or who I'm with."

I ignored her disapproving look, and hurried out.

*** 

Stuart Steele met me at the door of Bar Fish, and insisted I try a Neon Rainbow fishtail, which he told me was one of his own inventions. There was a little too much rum in it for my liking, but I persevered.

"So, Jill. What's the latest?"

"As I said on the phone, there isn't a latest. I'm very much at the beginning of my investigation."

"What about the police? Where are they with *their* investigation?"

"I can't speak for the police, Stuart."

"But Jack must tell you how things are progressing."

I didn't like the way this was going. I wasn't about to discuss anything that Jack had told me with Stuart.

"No, we don't discuss professional matters."

"Surely you must," he pressed.

"We don't. I can only report back on my own investigations. If you want any information from the police, you'll have to take that up with Jack."

Just then, I became aware of someone walking towards our table. It was Jack.

Oh bum!

"Hello, you two." He glanced from me to Stuart and back again.

"Hello, Jack," Stuart said. "We were just talking about you."

Oh bum, bum, bum!

"Were you *really*?" Jack glared at me. "Tell me more."

I said nothing, but Stuart did.

"I was just catching up on the Starr Fish case. I assume

you know that I've hired Jill to work on it for me?"

Jack glared at me again. "Actually I didn't know that. Jill must have forgotten to mention it to me."

"About that, Jack." I smiled as sweetly as I could.

"Never mind. I only popped in because I spotted you two through the window. I'm on my way to an important meeting. I'll catch up with you later, Stuart. And *you*, Jill."

I was really in trouble now.

After I'd finished my fishtail, I made my way to Ever A Wool Moment to see Kathy.

"I'm in deep water with Jack."

"Really? You do surprise me. What have you done now?"

"He caught me with Stuart Steele in Bar Fish."

"Oh dear." She laughed.

"It isn't funny. Stuart told him I was working on the Starr Fish case."

"Oh dear."

"Is that all you can say?"

"What do you expect? I warned you this would happen."

"You don't have to rub salt into the wound."

"What did Jack say?"

"That he'd catch up with me later."

"He's probably planning a romantic night in."

"Oh shut up, Kathy! You're no help."

# Chapter 15

Mad stopped by the office. Her hair was down again, and it looked pretty wild. Yet she was still wearing her librarian outfit.

"Another lunch hour and a half?"

"No, it's my half day. I've just finished."

"I didn't know you worked half days."

"Neither does the boss." She laughed. "I couldn't stand the thought of spending another minute in that place, so I said I had a dentist appointment. Anyway, I just dropped by to update you on Matthew Most. It seems he's well known to the authorities in Ghost Town. He's a bit of a naughty boy, our Matthew. His speciality seems to be stealing from stately homes in the human world. He fences the goods before taking his ill-gotten gains back to Ghost Town. He's been caught a couple of times and thrown in jail, but it doesn't seem to deter him for long. As soon as he's released, he's back to his old tricks again."

"I'd hardly call the colonel's house a stately home, but it's certainly a large property. And some of the items in there are probably worth quite a bit. Is there anything you can do about it?"

"I've had a word with my bosses back in Ghost Town, and they confirmed that there are a couple of warrants out on him already, so I don't even need to catch him red-handed. I can just ship him back to Ghost Town on the charges that are already outstanding."

"That's fantastic. Any idea when you'll be able to do it?"

"Seeing as I have the afternoon off I may as well get over there now."

"Thanks, Mad. I owe you."

"Funny you should say that."

Oh dear.

"You remember I mentioned my mum wanted you to come over for dinner?"

"Yeah?"

"Well, it's tonight. I realise it's short notice, but—"

"That's okay." What else could I say? I did owe her. "Look, don't take this the wrong way, but what's your mum's cooking like these days?"

I could still remember some of the slop Mad's mum had offered me when I was a kid. I'd come up with some great excuses to get out of it: *I have to get back home to shampoo my hamster, my dad is stuck up a ladder and needs me to help him.*

"She still can't cook to save her life. I wouldn't touch her stuff with a barge pole. But, she's got Nails to help her now. He used to work in a kitchen somewhere although he never says exactly where. He makes out it was a hotel, but I suspect it was probably in the nick."

"Prison?"

"I wouldn't be surprised, but to be fair, he's not a half bad cook. I've eaten a few meals that he's prepared."

"And?"

"And, I'm still here to tell the tale."

"High praise indeed."

"So, how about it? Seven-thirty at our house?"

"Sure. Why not? I'll see you then."

\*\*\*

Myrtle called to ask if I could get over to Middle Tweaking, so I jumped in the car, and made my way straight to the old watermill.

"Jill, come in." Myrtle greeted me at the door. "There are a couple of people here I'd like you to meet."

There were two old ladies sitting in the living room; they looked about the same age as Myrtle, but stranger characters you were unlikely to meet.

"Let me introduce you to two of my oldest friends. This is Celia Hodd."

Celia was no more than five-feet tall, although her stoop made her look even shorter. She was wearing what looked like men's boots, and walked with the aid of a stick which had a bulldog's head for a handle.

"Nice to meet you, Celia." I offered my hand.

"Call me Hodd. Everyone does." She had what sounded like a cockney accent, which seemed very out of place in rural Middle Tweaking.

"That's cos you *are* odd." The other woman laughed.

"Shut it, Jobbs!" Celia turned on her.

"Now, ladies." Myrtle stepped between the two of them. "What will Jill think of you?"

The two women continued to glare at one another.

"This is Constance Jobbs, Jill."

The second woman stepped forward. She was as tall as the other woman was short. It was difficult not to be distracted by the scar on her chin.

"Any friend of Turtle's is a friend of mine." Constance's grip was vice like. I was struggling to place her accent, but it might have been west country.

"Nice to meet you too, Constance."

"None of that Constance rubbish. Call me Jobbs. Everyone does."

"Or Jobbies," Hodd said.

"Only if they're tired of living." Jobbs turned on Hodd.

I know I can be slow on the uptake, but it was only then that it occurred to me: Celia Hodd and Constance Jobbs. Hodd Jobbs. So that's what Myrtle had meant when I thought she'd said odd jobs.

And *odd*, they most certainly were. I'd never come across a couple of old girls quite like them before.

Myrtle gestured for me to take a seat.

"Hodd, Jobbs and I go way back. We first met when we were—how should I put this? On opposite sides of the law."

"We're reformed characters now, though," Hodd assured me. "Aren't we, Jobbs?"

"Most of the time."

"Jobbs!" Myrtle shouted.

"Sorry. Yes, totally reformed."

"These two *ladies* occasionally do odd jobs for me." Myrtle laughed. "Get it? Hodd, Jobbs?"

"Oh yeah. That's very—err—good."

Why did anyone think making fun of people's names was funny? It was plain childish.

Myrtle continued. "When I came back to settle in Middle Tweaking, I heard that Hodd and Jobbs had fallen on hard times. And, although we'd often been adversaries, we'd become good friends over the years, so I invited them to come and live up here. They live in the old waterworks shed." She pointed to a building at the far end of her garden which I hadn't noticed before. "I had it renovated and converted some years back. Rather than pay rent, the ladies help me out with odd jobs from time to time."

"Help you out?"

"These two ladies have a certain *skillset* which can be useful in my investigations."

*Skillset?* Before I could ask what she meant, she continued.

"The other day, Jill, you mentioned you'd like to get a look at the murder scene."

"That's right. Do you think there's any chance that we'll be able to get in?"

"Let me put it this way. If we were to ask the police, I'm pretty sure the answer would be a resounding 'no'. But there's more than one way to — "

Paws over your ears, Winky!

Myrtle continued. "My two friends here will be able to get us inside, I'm sure. Won't you ladies?"

"No problem, Turtle." Hodd grinned.

"Piece of cake." Jobbs agreed.

"Are you talking about breaking in?" I asked.

"*Breaking in* is rather an emotive expression," Myrtle said. "Let's just say they'll be able to facilitate our entry."

"Is that a good idea?"

"It's the only way we're going to get a chance to take a look around."

If I'd been working the case alone, I'd have used magic to get inside, but that wasn't an option. I was more than a little worried at the thought of Hodd and Jobbs breaking in.

"Off you go, you two," Myrtle said. "We'll give you five minutes. Will that be long enough?"

"More than enough." Hodd was already on her way to the door.

"Piece of cake," Jobbs said.

"Just make sure you're not seen. Jill and I will follow

you over there in five."

"Consider it done, Turtle," Hodd said. "Nice to meet you, Jill."

"You too."

"They're rather a strange couple, aren't they?" I commented, after they'd left.

"Hearts of gold—both of them. In their day, they were responsible for a good proportion of the burglaries in the West End. They saw themselves as sort of Robin Hood characters. Robbing from the rich and giving to the poor."

"The poor?"

"Themselves. But those days are behind them now, apart from the occasional job for me."

After five minutes, Myrtle beckoned me to follow her. She led the way through the village, and around the back of the post office. There was no sign of Hodd or Jobbs, but lo and behold, the back door was open. There was no sign that it had been forced, so I could only surmise that the ladies had picked the lock.

"Come on, Jill. Before someone sees us." Myrtle led the way upstairs to the flat where Madge Hick had lived. "You take the kitchen; that's where her body was found. I'll take a look in the bedroom."

There was no obvious sign that a murder had taken place in that very spot only days before. I had no idea what I was looking for, but felt sure I'd recognise it when I saw it. After a few minutes, Myrtle called to me. "Jill, come and look at this."

In the drawer of the bedside cabinet was a pile of papers. When I took a closer look, I realised what they were: Lottery slips. Lots of them.

"They go back years," Myrtle said. "Every week, the

same numbers."

"So Madge was telling the truth when she said she'd bought a ticket every week."

"It looks like it. Wouldn't you know the numbers came up the one week she forgot."

"She could easily have proven she wasn't cheating because she'd kept all these tickets. I wonder why she didn't say something?"

"Maybe she felt the others should have taken her at her word, and that she shouldn't have to prove anything. It's all very tragic."

Myrtle moved on to the living room, while I continued to look around the kitchen. Out of the window, I could see the beer garden on the roof of The Old Trout, which was only a few yards away. An hour later, we called it a day. We'd found nothing of any consequence.

\*\*\*

From Middle Tweaking, I went straight back to my flat. I wasn't sure what to wear for dinner at Mad's mother's house. I suspected that whatever I chose I'd be overdressed. As a kid, I'd always been apprehensive about going to Mad's house. Her mother had always been a little strange — and yes, I realise that's rich coming from me. She'd delighted in embarrassing me at every opportunity. Still, I didn't have to worry about that now we were both adults.

Who was I trying to kid?

The man who answered the door looked out to lunch. He never once made eye contact with me; he was too busy tapping away on his phone.

"Good evening." I tried to catch his attention.

Tap, tap, tap.

"I'm Jill Gooder."

Tap, tap, tap.

"Madeline invited me."

"Come in." He didn't bother looking up from his phone. "They're in the living room." He pointed the way, and then walked off in the opposite direction—towards the kitchen.

Mad was by herself. "Is that Nails?" I said, in a low voice.

"That's him. Once seen, never forgotten. No matter how hard I try."

"He didn't say much. He was too busy on his phone."

"Think yourself lucky he wasn't biting his nails. He never stops."

The more I heard, the more I was looking forward to dinner.

"Anyway, I've got a bone to pick with you, Jill Gooder."

"What have I done now?"

"I went to the colonel's house this afternoon."

"Was there a problem?"

"Only that practically everyone up there was stark naked."

"Oh, yeah." I laughed. "I forgot to mention that."

"You kind of did, didn't you? I didn't know where to put my face. The only person who was wearing any clothes was the old butler who let me in. He told me I'd find the owner on the back porch. There were half-a-dozen of them playing volleyball—all stark naked! Then the guy who owns the house got off the lounger, naked as you'll like, and shook my hand. I almost died of embarrassment."

"I'm really sorry, Mad." I said through tears of laughter.

"Yeah, you look it."

"Did you manage to get things sorted out?"

"I told the owner that I was from Washbridge Better Homes magazine."

"Is there such a thing?"

"I doubt it. Anyway, he was only too pleased to let me take a look around. I bumped into the colonel while I was there, and he pointed me in the direction of Matthew Most, who was eyeing up the silverware in the dining room. He wasn't very happy to see me."

"Did you catch him?"

"Of course I did. He tried to make a run for it, but he was way too slow. He's back in Ghost Town now. The colonel won't have any more trouble from Matthew Most—not for a few years, at least."

"Thanks, Mad. I owe you."

"You definitely do. Big time."


"Dinner's burnt." Mad's mother, Delilah, came storming in. "It's Nails' fault. I told him to watch that pie, but he was too busy playing on his stupid phone. Sorry about this, Jill. How are you, anyway?"

"Okay, thanks, Mrs Lane."

"I've told you. Call me Deli. Mrs Lane makes me sound ancient. Have you got yourself a fella yet?"

"Mum!" Mad yelled.

"I'm only asking. So, have you, Jill?"

"Yes, I am seeing someone."

"That's more than this one is doing." She gestured to Mad. "She's never likely to either, not the way she dresses. No fella wants to see a woman dressed in a woollen two-piece. I keep telling her to wear something that makes the most of what she's got—you know—show a bit of cleavage and a bit of leg."

"Mother!" Mad's face was red with embarrassment. "What did I tell you?"

"Jill doesn't mind, do you, Jill?"

I managed a smile.

"I've ordered in some pizza. It should be here in twenty minutes. I'll go and shave my legs while we're waiting."

"I'm sorry about that," Mad said, once her mother had gone.

"It's just like the good old days."

"I've got to get my own place. If I stay here much longer, I might do something I regret."

It was almost thirty minutes later when a spotty, young guy arrived with the pizza. It was surprisingly good, but I would have enjoyed it even more had it not been for the fact that Nails was picking at his toe nails all through the meal. Every time Delilah yelled at him, he stopped, but only for a few minutes.

"So what's your fella's name?" Delilah said, through a mouthful of pizza.

"Jack." I ducked to avoid a low-flying toe nail.

"You should bring him over to meet us some time."

"Yeah, sure."

"When?"

"Soon." The day after hell freezes over.

# Chapter 16

These bean bags were such a stupid idea. I was in Beans—waiting for Jack. He'd called and asked if we could meet up. I'd suggested Coffee Triangle, but he'd reminded me it was drum day, so not exactly conducive to conversation. He'd said we needed to talk, but when I'd pressed him about what in particular, he'd been evasive. I had a horrible feeling this was not going to end well.

I was desperately trying to balance on the stupid bean bag, and drink my coffee at the same time. Whoever had come up with this idea had to have been crazy. When Jack walked in, our eyes met, and I thought I detected the hint of a smile. Maybe things weren't as bad as I'd thought. Even so, it felt like forever while he got himself a coffee. I just wanted to know what this was all about.

"Maybe this place wasn't such a good idea," he said, almost spilling his drink as he got down onto the bean bag next to me.

"What's up? Is everything okay?" Fingers crossed.

"I thought we needed to clear the air."

"Look, I'm sorry about—"

"Can I say my piece before you start with the apologies?"

"Yeah, sorry. I mean—err—yeah, go on."

"Look, Jill. I realise you have a job to do, and I know that from time to time our paths are going to cross, professionally, but I can't have you involved with cases unless I know about it. If nothing else, it's embarrassing when I hear from one of my colleagues that my girlfriend is working on a case behind my back."

He just called me his girlfriend, not *ex*-girlfriend. Maybe there was still hope.

"You're absolutely right. I should have told you. I know it's no excuse, but Stuart Steele approached me out of the blue, and asked if I'd look into Starr Fish's murder."

"And at that point you should have done what?" Jack prompted.

This was beginning to feel like an interrogation, and my instincts were to fight back, but I still had enough sense to realise that wasn't a good idea.

"I should have mentioned it to you."

"But instead, you pumped me for information."

"I wouldn't say that."

"What would you call it? You asked me questions about the case without mentioning you were working on it."

"Yeah but—"

"But nothing, Jill. If we're to make a go of this, that can't happen again. If you're working on any case that the police are involved with, you have to tell me."

"Okay, but that doesn't mean you can tell me I can't work the case."

"I wouldn't do that."

"Of course you would. You do it every time."

"Okay. I'm prepared to accept that you're free to work on whatever cases you wish, but only on condition that you tell me. Agreed?"

"That's fair. Agreed. So are we good now?"

"Yes, but there's one more thing."

"Go on."

"I need you to promise that you won't lie to me ever again. About anything."

What? My whole life was a lie—in particular the fact that I was a witch, and could never tell Jack.

"Jill?"

"Yeah, of course. I promise."

Oh bum!

***

It was time to go back to Middle Tweaking, yet again. It was a pity I couldn't just magic myself around the human world. The truth was, I probably could, now that I had the additional powers I'd inherited from Magna, but it just didn't feel right. I tried to keep the magic I used in Washbridge to a bare minimum because I ran the risk of being exposed as a witch. I was even more conscious of the danger of giving myself away now I was seeing Jack.

Myrtle was waiting for me at the old watermill.

"Are you okay, Jill? You look a bit down in the dumps. Not man trouble is it?"

"No, of course not."

"We'd better get going. I told Brendan Breeze that we'd be with him five minutes ago."

"I'm sorry I'm late. There were roadworks in Lower Tweaking."

"It's okay. They're always digging that road up."

Brendan Breeze had the look of a sad puppy, and just as Myrtle had warned, smelled of fish. He barely said a word when he answered the door.

"I still can't believe it." His eyes looked bloodshot as though he'd been crying for a long time. 'I can't believe Madge is dead."

"It came as a shock to us all." Myrtle reassured him.

"You know that Madge and I used to be an item, I suppose."

"Yes, but the way I heard it, you dumped her."

"It's true. I did. I was an idiot; I should never have done it. Madge and I were good together. I don't know what I was thinking."

"From what I hear, you traded her in for a younger model." Myrtle was taking no prisoners now.

"You're right. I'm just a stupid old man."

"You're surely not waiting for me to disagree, are you Brendan?"

"No, I know I am. I allowed my eyes to wander, and convinced myself that Suzy was interested in me. I was stupid. She was only after what she could get. I bought her clothes, jewellery, handbags, all sorts of things. That's all she wanted me for. When the money began to run out, she found herself a new boyfriend, and left me in the lurch. I tried to make it up with Madge, but she didn't want to know."

"Can you blame her?"

"Of course not. It's all I deserved."

"You got that much right. Didn't you even accuse her of trying to sabotage your business?"

"I don't know what I was thinking." He shook his head. "Madge would never have done anything like that. Not in a million years. It's just that things had started to go wrong with the business, and Suzy was two-timing me with some young fellow. I think the stress must have got to me, and I just lashed out. It was crazy. I should never have said the things I said. If I could take them back now, I would." He started towards the door. "Would you excuse me for a minute? I've got a thumping headache. I need to get some tablets."

When he had disappeared into the kitchen, I turned to

Myrtle and said, "What do you think?"

"Words are cheap. It's easy for him to be sorry now. Even so, my gut feeling is he's telling the truth."

I nodded. If this was all an act, it was a really good one.

When he came back, he was still rubbing his forehead. "Sorry about that. I've got one heck of a hangover. There was a lock-in at The Old Trout last night."

"I thought those had been stopped," Myrtle said.

"They were for a long time. You know why, I assume?"

Myrtle shook her head.

"Trevor used to run them every night. Madge lived right next door, and had to get up early for the post office. The late night drinkers were waking her up when they left the pub in the early hours of the morning. She complained to Trevor, and when he did nothing about it, she took it to the police. They put a stop to the lock-ins. They would probably have turned a blind eye if Madge hadn't complained."

"What did you think about the lottery situation," Myrtle asked.

"There's no way Madge would have cheated the others. It was obviously a genuine mistake. But, I was so blinded by rage at the time, that I sided with those who accused her of cheating. I'm ashamed; I should have stood up for her."

As the minutes passed, Brendan became less and less responsive. He was obviously still suffering from the previous night's drinking.

"Okay Brendan." Myrtle stood up. "I think we'd better leave it there. If I have any more questions, I'll come and see you again when you're not so hung over."

"Yeah, okay. I'm sorry about this." He showed us to the

door. "I hope you find out who murdered Madge. She didn't deserve to meet her end like that."

When we got outside, I asked Myrtle what she'd made of Brendan.

"He seemed genuinely sorry about the way he'd treated Madge, but I was more interested in what he had to say about the lock-ins."

"I wasn't really sure what that was all about."

"With all the clubs and late-night bars in the city, there's probably no need for lock-ins. But out here in the sticks, it's different. The pubs are expected to close by eleven or eleven-thirty at the latest. There's only the one pub in Middle Tweaking, and the truth is that a lot of people want to keep drinking long after that—especially at the weekend. Trevor satisfied that demand by holding lock-ins."

"At the risk of sounding stupid, what exactly is a lock-in?"

"At 'closing time', the landlord locks the doors as though the pub is closed. Those remaining in the pub after that time are supposed to be friends of the landlord who have been invited for a drink, with no money changing hands. In reality, it's just the regular customers who have stayed behind to drink and spend money."

"And according to Brendan, Madge got the lock-ins closed down."

"Exactly, and that's what caught my attention," Myrtle said. "Trevor won't have been very happy that Madge cut off a major part of his income."

"Are you suggesting that could be a motive for murder?"

"Probably not, but I do think we should have another word with our friend, Trevor."

"Do you want to do that now?"

"No time like the present."

"Why don't you ask him how he felt about Madge getting the lock-ins closed down while I take a closer look around the pub."

"That's a good idea, Jill. I'll go in first, and see if I can get him to talk to me in the back. You give it five minutes, then come in and take a good look around. See if you come up with anything of interest."

I watched through the window as Myrtle approached Trevor who was behind the bar. They spoke for a while, and then disappeared into the back. That was my cue.

"Morning, madam." The young woman behind the bar greeted me. "What can I get for you?"

"Could I just get a coffee, please?"

"Certainly. Cappuccino, latte, flat white?"

"Latte please."

"Regular or decaf?"

"Regular."

"Skinny or—"

"Just give me a cup of tea, please." Life was too short.

"Okay, I'll bring it over to you."

There were framed photos on all of the walls. The majority were of fishing competitions. Trevor Total featured prominently in every photo. In most he was either holding a large fish or an even larger trophy. When I studied them in more detail, I could see that most of the trophies had been won for fly fishing. In fact, many of the photos referred to Trevor (the Fly) Total.

"There you are, madam." The barmaid put the tray on

the table. "Help yourself to milk and sugar."

Before I could take a drink, Myrtle reappeared, and gestured for me to follow her out of the pub.

"Did you find anything, Jill?"

"Not really. I discovered that Trevor is an expert fly fisherman, but I don't think that helps us. What about you? Did you come up with anything?"

"He didn't appreciate my line of questioning. As soon as I got onto the subject of the lock-ins, his demeanour changed, and he became very defensive. He said there'd never been any trouble with the lock-ins, and the only reason he'd stopped them was because he'd been feeling the stress of working so many hours."

"I thought it was Madge who had got them closed down?"

"I put that to him, but he insisted that wasn't the case."

"Brendan seemed to think it was. They can't both be right."

Myrtle said nothing for the longest moment; she was obviously deep in thought. "I have a hunch, but to prove it, I'm going to need the services of our friends Hodd and Jobbs."

"Another break-in?"

"Please, Jill." Myrtle tutted. "Such crude terminology. The ladies wouldn't approve."

"Sorry. What exactly do you have in mind?"

"All in good time. Can you come back tonight for the lock-in?"

"Sure. What time?"

"Can you get here for about ten-thirty?"

"No problem. What's the plan?"

"Once the lock-in is in full swing, I'll need you to keep

Trevor occupied while Hodd and Jobbs do their thing. Can you do that?"

"Sure, I'll see you tonight."

# Chapter 17

Kathy had invited me over because Peter and his new employee were going to be working late. As I was already in the city centre, I thought I'd pop into Ever A Wool Moment to meet her there.

When I arrived at the wool shop, I noticed two familiar faces in the tea room. It was Grandma with Miles Best. They were enjoying a beverage, and seemed to be having a good old chinwag. Grandma was actually smiling.

I grabbed Kathy. "What's going on with those two?"

"They're BFFs now."

"Grandma and Miles Best? Are you serious?"

"Yes, ever since the incident with the Never-ending Wool, he's been coming over here to chat with your grandmother. At first, she wasn't very enthusiastic, but he seems to have won her over. He does have a certain charm about him."

"He must have if he's managed to talk Grandma around."

"From the few snippets of conversation I've caught, it sounds as though they're discussing a number of joint ventures. They've been talking about initiatives whereby they can cross-sell between the two shops."

I had to hand it to Miles. Ever since he'd begged me to get Grandma to reverse the spell on the Never-ending Wool, he'd kept his promise to change his ways. Not only had he closed down Best P.I. Services, but he'd also offered to share his circus acts with the twins, and now he was looking to go into joint ventures with Grandma. It was such a complete turnaround that I wasn't sure what to make of it. Had the leopard really changed its spots or was he just luring us into a false sense of security?

After Miles and Grandma had left, I waited until Kathy had locked up. One of her friends had collected the kids from school, so they were already home when we arrived.

"Auntie Jill! Auntie Jill!" Lizzie came running up to me. "Don't forget, it's my talent competition soon. You are coming, aren't you?"

"Of course she's coming," Kathy said, before I could come up with an excuse. "You've been looking forward to it, haven't you, Auntie Jill?"

"Yes, I'm counting the minutes."

Thump, bang, thump, bang, thump, bang. Mikey appeared with his drum.

"I thought you weren't allowed to play the drum in the house?"

"I keep telling you, Auntie Jill, it's not my birthday yet. When I get my new drum kit, I have to play it in the shop."

"You can't expect your Auntie Jill to remember when your birthday is, Mikey." Kathy gave me *that* look. "After all, she has so many nephews and nieces to keep track of."

I ignored the cutting (but thoroughly deserved) remark.

"Have you heard any more about the Madge Hick murder?" Kathy asked, after she'd given the kids their microwave pizza (hmm, yummy cardboard!)

"Didn't I mention it? We're working on the case."

"No you didn't mention it. And who is '*we*'?"

"I've been working on it with Myrtle Turtle from Middle Tweaking."

"Myrtle Turtle?" Kathy laughed.

"She's an amateur investigator."

"Like you, then?"

"Cheek. I'll have you know I'm the consummate professional."

"I thought you preferred to work solo?"

"Generally I do, but Myrtle knows her stuff. And besides, she knows the locals. I'm going over there tonight. We're going to a lock-in at The Old Trout."

"A lock-in? Isn't that just an excuse to drink until the early hours of the morning?"

"Technically, yes. But that's not why we're going."

"Hmm? According to you."

Just then, the front door opened.

"It's me," Peter shouted. "I've brought someone with me for dinner, I hope you don't mind."

Kathy looked at me, and rolled her eyes. "I hate it when he does this. He'll expect me to magic up dinner from somewhere, with no warning at all."

Peter looked hot and sweaty after his day's endeavours. "Jill, I didn't realise you were here. Look Kathy, I'm sorry I didn't give you any warning, but as we've been working late, I told Jethro he could have dinner with us."

Jethro? It couldn't be. Could it?

I only had to glance at Kathy's expression to have my answer. She was practically salivating. It was the man who until recently had worked for Aunt Lucy. The man who was adored by every female who saw him, including the twins and Aunt Lucy. Not me though, obviously. I'm not so shallow. He'd given up his gardening job to pursue a career as a male model, and the last time I'd seen him had been in 'Hunk', where he'd been part of a male dance troupe.

He glanced across at me, and I saw a hint of recognition

in his eyes. Neither of us said anything to indicate that we knew one another, and obviously, Peter and Kathy had no idea that he was actually a wizard.

"This is Jethro," Peter said. "Jethro, this is Kathy, my wife, and this is Jill, Kathy's sister."

"Pleased to meet you both." He shook our hands.

Kathy took forever to release his hand; she was well and truly smitten.

"We'll get washed up while you make us something to eat." Peter gestured for Jethro to follow him. "Burger and chips maybe?"

"Of course." Kathy whimpered. "Will burger be enough for you, Jethro? I can do something else if you'd prefer it?"

"Burger will be fine, thanks."

Once the two men had left, I turned to Kathy. "*Will burger be enough for you, Jethro?*" I mocked.

"What?"

"You soon changed your tune. One minute, you're moaning about Peter bringing someone home for dinner, and the next you're fawning all over him."

"I was not *fawning.*"

"Do me a favour. That was world-class fawning."

"Did you see him, though?"

"What about him?" I shrugged.

"Are you blind? He's possibly the most handsome man I've ever seen. And what a body!"

"I can't say I noticed. I'm far more interested in a man's personality than his looks or physique."

"Of course you are. Do you think I should get changed for dinner?"

"No, just make the burgers."

By the time I left, Kathy had changed into her best

dress. It was pathetic, I'd never go to all that trouble just to impress a man.

What do you mean my date with Luther? That was totally different. Obviously.

*** 

Just after nine, I drove over to Middle Tweaking where I checked in with Myrtle, to make sure that the plans hadn't changed. She confirmed I was to ensure I was included in the 'lock-in', and that I should keep Trevor distracted once the doors had been locked.

"Hello again," Trevor greeted me. "You're becoming a bit of a regular."

"I'm actually thinking of buying a property in the village, so I thought I should stay over for a few days."

Once I had my drink, I found a quiet corner, and waited. Just before eleven, Trevor came over.

"It's Jill, isn't it?"

"That's right."

"Look Jill, the pub will be closing shortly, but we're having what's known locally, as a 'lock-in'."

"Oh? What's that?" Again, with the Oscar worthy performance.

"A few regulars stay behind, and carry on drinking after the doors have been locked. Seeing as you're thinking of moving here, you're welcome to stay, if you like?"

"Thanks. That's very kind. I wouldn't mind staying a little longer if that's all right."

Only a couple of people left before the doors were locked; everyone else simply carried on as before. Myrtle and her sidekicks would be putting their plan into action about now, so I needed to make sure Trevor didn't disturb them.

"Trevor, could I get a lime and soda, please?"

"Are you sure? Wouldn't you like something a little stronger?"

"No, thanks. Lime and soda will be fine. I see you're something of a fisherman." I pointed to the photos on the wall.

"Yes, all my life really. Are you interested in fishing, Jill?"

"My father was a keen fisherman, and he used to take me from time to time."

"Did he go in for competitions?"

"No. He wasn't all that good. It was just his way of relaxing. You've obviously had a lot of success, though."

"Yes, indeed."

"What's that photo over there?" I pointed.

"That was when I won the cup for fly-fishing in Cumbria in 1997."

"And that one?"

And that's how it continued for the next three quarters of an hour. I pointed to a photo, and Trevor bored me to death telling me where, when and how he'd won the cup. He only broke off occasionally to serve drinks to the other customers who had remained behind.

My brain was about to melt and come pouring out of my nose. I was so bored. The sheer effort of trying to look interested was beginning to wear me down.

Suddenly, from a door behind the bar, Myrtle appeared.

Trevor turned around, obviously surprised. "Myrtle? Where did you come from?"

"Upstairs."

"What were you doing up there? How did you get in?"

Just then, there was a knock on the door.

"I think you should get that, Trevor," Myrtle said.

He glanced back and forth between Myrtle and the door—not really knowing what to do. There was another knock—louder this time. That made his mind up.

It was Sergeant Charlie Cross. "Can I come in Trevor?"

"This isn't what it looks like. Just a few friends over for drinks."

"I'm not here about the lock-in. I'm here to arrest you for the murder of Madge Hick."

"What? Is this some kind of joke?"

"It's hardly a joking matter." He turned to Myrtle. "Ready?"

"Yes. Follow me."

"Wait!" Trevor shouted. "You can't go up there."

"This warrant says I can." The sergeant flashed a sheet of paper at Trevor. It could have been a shopping list, for all I could tell.

Sergeant Cross took hold of Trevor's arm, and led him to the door where Myrtle was waiting. She gestured for me to follow. When we got to the top of the stairs, Myrtle stopped, and said, "You almost got away with it, Trevor."

"Got away with what? I don't know what you're talking about."

"Of course you do." She pressed one of the wooden panels, which then slid open to reveal a 'secret' room. Inside, there were rows of shelves on which were glass cages containing all manner of creepy crawlies and reptiles. It was incredibly hot inside the cramped room.

"After you left your job at the zoo, you missed the

exotic creatures that you'd looked after, didn't you?"

"What of it? There's no law against keeping these."

"Actually, I think you'll find there is," Sergeant Cross said. "I suspect some of these are dangerous, and require a special licence. I've checked, and you don't have one. You probably knew you'd never be granted a licence to keep them above a pub."

"I look after them; they're all perfectly healthy."

"I'm sure they are," Myrtle said. "But, that's not really the point, is it? My guess is some of the snakes have a lethal venom. I suspect that if you were to mix the venom of several of these, you'd probably end up with a poison similar to that found in Madge Hick's bloodstream."

"That's just wild speculation." Trevor protested.

"Maybe, but once the scientists know which snakes they're dealing with, it shouldn't be difficult to test that theory."

"And how am I meant to have administered the poison? I was in the pub all night."

"You're right, of course," Myrtle conceded. "But that's where you were clever. Follow me." She led the way to the beer garden on the roof.

"It's a great view from here, isn't it Trevor? Look, that's Madge's kitchen. It's easy to spot; it's the room with the window which is half open."

"What are you suggesting? That I threw a poisoned dart at her? Or maybe used a blowpipe?" He laughed, but it was unconvincing. "I might be on the pub's dart team, but I'm not that good a shot. And besides, the dart would have been found."

Myrtle smiled the smile of a woman who knew she had her man.

"You didn't need a dart, Trevor. You used a rod and line. You coated the hook with venom, and then cast the line. You're an expert—the photos downstairs are proof of that. Getting the line through Madge's window would have been a trivial matter for you. Once the hook had delivered its poison you simply pulled it back."

The colour drained from Trevor's face. He knew the game was up.

"Trevor Total, I'm arresting you for the murder of Madge Hick." The sergeant clamped handcuffs around Trevor's wrists, and led him away.

"That was brilliant, Myrtle," I said, once we were outside.

"I've got you to thank for it, Jill."

"Me? What did I do?"

"It was when you mentioned the fly-fishing that it all started to make sense. Madge tried to tell us who murdered her. That's why she wrote 'FL' in the flour. She knew Trevor was known as 'The Fly'. And, do you remember that Harry complained about the smell of old frogs? That was the exotic animals. From there, it wasn't difficult to put two and two together. Trevor had the means to deliver the poison—casting a line through that open window would have been child's play for him. I just had to work out where the animals were. Once Hodd and Jobbs were able to get me inside, the smell soon led me to them."

"Myrtle, if you ever decide to come and live in Washbridge, there's a job waiting for you. I think we'd make a great team."

"I'm too old for all that. That's a young person's game. I think I'll stay in Middle Tweaking; the pace of life here is more suited to me. Besides which, what would Hodd and Jobbs do without me?"

"Well, thanks again. You've taught me a great deal."

"Not at all Jill, I've learnt a lot from you too. Keep in touch."

"I will."

"Bye then."

# Chapter 18

The next morning, I hadn't been in the office very long when I felt a bit of a chill. Sure enough, moments later, the colonel and Priscilla appeared. Thankfully, they were both dressed, so I didn't have to avert my eyes.

"Hi, Colonel. Hi, Priscilla. How's things?"

"Much better, Jill, thank you," the colonel said. "And it's all down to you, again. I'm pleased to report that Matthew Most is no longer causing us problems up at the house."

"So I understand. Mad dropped in and told me that she'd sent him packing back to Ghost Town. Apparently, there were already several warrants out for him."

"He was a nasty piece of work altogether." The colonel glanced at Priscilla who was remarkably quiet. "We're glad to be rid of him, aren't we, Cilla?"

"Yes, Briggsy."

Unless I was very much mistaken, Cilla didn't seem quite as pleased with the outcome as the colonel obviously was.

"You really must let us thank you properly, Jill," the colonel said. "Why don't you come up to the house for dinner some time?"

"Is that possible? What about the new owners?"

"They hardly ever venture into the west wing. We've more or less made that our home now, haven't we, Cilla?"

"Yes, Briggsy. It's really very private up there." She seemed a little brighter now. "We'd love to have you join us for dinner."

"But what about—err—I mean—how do you manage to prepare meals?"

"That's the other piece of news I have for you." The colonel beamed with obvious delight. "You remember Mrs Burnbridge, don't you?"

"Yes, of course. Is she enjoying her retirement?"

"That's the thing. Her retirement didn't last very long."

"Oh dear, you don't mean—"

"No, nothing like that. She's perfectly fine. The other day, I overheard the new owner mention that he could do with a housekeeper/cook. He was toying with the idea of advertising, so I conveniently left some papers on his desk: Mrs Burnbridge's employment records."

"And he contacted her?"

"He certainly did. Mrs Burnbridge was delighted to get back to the house. Retirement didn't suit her; she was bored to tears."

"Have you managed to make contact with her?"

"Yes indeed."

"She didn't die of fright, then?"

"No. She seemed to take it all in her stride. I should have known she would. And, of course, I introduced her to Cilla. You and Mrs Burnbridge get on famously, don't you, Cilla?"

"Oh yes, she's such a lovely old dear."

"How does it work with the meals?"

"Primarily, of course, Mrs Burnbridge is working for the new owner, but she also makes meals for us from time to time. If you were to join us for dinner, you'd actually be enjoying Mrs Burnbridge's cooking."

"In that case, I'd love to. Will Mrs Burnbridge be joining us?"

"I don't see why not. That's a jolly good idea. What about bringing your young man too?"

"I don't think that's going to work, unfortunately, Colonel."

"Have you and he fallen out?"

"Nothing like that. It's just that he doesn't know ghosts exist, and I'd rather keep it that way."

"Of course. I understand. Not to worry. I'll be in touch to arrange a date."

***

Now the case in Middle Tweaking had been resolved, I could focus all my attention on the Starr Fish murder. I'd arranged to meet with Maureen James, who was Scott Venus's old girlfriend. Of course, when she'd gone out with him, he hadn't been 'Scott Venus'; he'd been plain old Alan Smith. Maureen flat-shared in an apartment block, which was close to Beans.

The woman who answered the door was very spotty. I don't mean she had acne; everything she was wearing was covered in spots: A polka-dot dress, grey tights covered with little red spots, and in her hair, a yellow ribbon covered in blue spots.

"Hello?" She was obviously surprised to see me. "I'm just on my way out."

"Are you Maureen James?"

"No, I'm Dotty."

I laughed.

"What's wrong?"

"Dotty?"

"Yeah, that's my name."

"But, the dots—you are covered—never mind. Is Maureen in?"

"She's in her bedroom. Do you want me to get her for you?"

"Yes, please."

"Who shall I say wants to speak to her?"

"Tell her it's Jill Gooder. I'm a private investigator."

"I bet that's exciting! I've always wanted to be a private investigator. I think I'd be really good at undercover work."

"Really?" She wouldn't be at all conspicuous in that outfit.

"Anyway, I'll just go and get Maureen." Moments later, I heard her shout, "Mo! Mo! There's a private investigator here to see you."

There was a muffled sound, and moments later, Dotty came back.

"She's in bed. She always sleeps late, but I think she's getting up now. Sorry, but I have to get going."

I waited by the door, but after five minutes, there was still no sign of the elusive Maureen, so I stepped inside.

"Hello? Hello? Maureen?"

Still no sign, so I found what appeared to be the bedroom, and knocked on the door. There was no answer, so I pushed it open. There was someone under the duvet; I pulled it back just enough to reveal a head.

"What do you want?" The woman's pyjamas were covered in pears, apples, oranges, grapes, and all manner of fruit. She looked at me through half-open eyes.

"Who are you? What do you want?"

"My name's Jill Gooder. I'm a private investigator."

"No thanks. I've already got some."

"I'm not selling anything."

"Bye."

"No, don't go back to sleep." I shook her gently until she opened her eyes again.

"Who are you?"

Oh, boy. This was going to take some time.

I eventually managed to get her out of bed. But I had to make her a cup of coffee because without it, I wasn't convinced she'd stay awake.

We were in the kitchen.

"Who did you say you were again?"

"Jill Gooder, private investigator."

"What do you want?"

"I believe you used to go out with Alan Smith?"

"Yeah, I did."

"I assume that was before he became Scott Venus."

"Scott Venus?" She scoffed. "I told him that was a stupid name."

"You and he are no longer an item?"

She shook her head.

"Did it end before or after he went on the reality TV show?"

"Afterwards. We were fine before he got involved with all that. When he said he was submitting an application for the show, it never crossed my mind that he might actually get in. And even when he did, I didn't think anything would come of it."

"When did he change his name?"

"He'd heard that some of the other contestants were changing their names before they went in. He reckoned if he didn't do the same, he wouldn't have a chance. He said no one would vote for Alan Smith when there were contestants like Starr Fish in there. I tried to persuade him not to do it, but he wouldn't listen."

"Did he split up with you as soon as he was voted out of the competition?"

"No, not straight away. I'd half expected it because I'd seen him flirting with Starr Fish on TV. I didn't know whether that was real or just for the benefit of the cameras. But, when he came out, we seemed to be okay for a while. Until Chaz Taylor stuck his oar in."

"Chaz? His manager?"

"Yeah. He signed them all up before the show began. A real conman if ever there was one. Anyway, he had the bright idea that if Scott—Scott? Listen to me, *I'm* calling him Scott now. Anyway, Chaz had the bright idea that if Alan and Starr pretended they were a couple then the press would take more interest in them."

"From what I understand, it didn't quite work out like that."

"No, it didn't. The press were only interested in Starr. Poor old Alan got his nose pushed out."

"What about you? You must resent Alan for dumping you like that."

"I wasn't very pleased at the time, but I'm over it now. I'm glad I found out what he was like before we got too involved. I've seen a couple of guys since then, so he's history now."

"Do you think Alan could have murdered Starr Fish?"

"Alan? Murder someone? Not in a million years. I don't think Alan's your man."

\*\*\*

As I walked back to the office, I noticed a new shop which I hadn't seen before. The last time I'd been on that street, the shop had been empty. Someone had obviously spent quite a bit of money on it because the frontage had been completely revamped. It was the sign that caught my attention: 'Love You To Death Dating Agency'.

Surely not. It couldn't be, could it? I was probably going to regret this, but curiosity got the better of me.

The young woman behind the reception desk greeted me with more of a frown than a smile.

"I just popped in out of curiosity. Have you been open long?"

"No, we only opened last week. Aren't you a witch?"

"That's right."

"I'm very sorry, but I don't think we can help you. We're a dating agency which is exclusively for Grim Reapers."

"That's what I thought. Tell me, is the owner by any chance James Keeper?"

"Yes. Do you know Jim?"

"Our paths have crossed. In fact, he discussed the idea of this dating agency with me and Hilary from Love Spell."

"Hilary has been helping Jim with the launch."

"It's nice to see that he got the business off the ground. Is Jim in today?"

"No, he's at a meeting with the accountant."

"Oh, well. Never mind. How's business so far?"

"It's early days, but we've already had about half a dozen Reapers sign up."

"I didn't realise there were so many in Washbridge."

"There's always a demand for Reapers."

"I guess so."

"There aren't any other specialised Reaper dating

agencies, so Jim has cornered the market."

"How does it work exactly? Do you pair up Grim Reapers with humans?"

"No, Jim considered doing that. But, based on his own experience with humans, he decided it wouldn't work."

"He's probably right." I thought back to my date with him.

"So he decided the agency would be exclusively for Grim Reapers."

"But don't you get people just wandering in off the street?"

"Not many. We get the odd person who, like yourself, is curious. If they're a sup, we just explain the agency is only for Reapers. If it's a human, it's a little more difficult. We can hardly say that we don't accept humans, so we allow them to sign up. The first month is free, but they never hear from us again, so they don't end up paying us any money."

"That's quite ingenious. What about you? Have you used the agency?"

"No, I have no need for it. I already have a boyfriend."

"Another Reaper?"

"Yes."

"I see. I'm sorry, I didn't catch your name."

"I'm Kim. Kim Neaper."

"No, seriously, what's your real name?"

"That *is* my real name."

"So you're Kim Neaper, the Grim Reaper?"

"Oh? I see what you mean. It rhymes, doesn't it? It never occurred to me."

O—kay.

"Well, give my regards to Jim. Tell him I'll pop in again

some time to see how things are going."

# Chapter 19

"Grandma? What a nice surprise."

Did you see how I did that? I actually sounded like I meant it. I was getting really good at this.

"Don't pretend you're pleased to see me," she barked.

Seems I wasn't as good as I thought I was.

"To what do I owe this *pleasure*?"

"It's time for your lesson."

"Sorry?"

She sighed. "Your lesson. It is time for it. Which bit of that don't you understand?"

"But Grandma, don't you remember? I got into the sealed room at Candlefield Museum of Witchcraft. I've inherited all of Magna's knowledge and power. Surely I don't still need lessons, do I?"

"I said it was time for *your* lesson. I did not say it was time for you to *take* a lesson. You're *giving* the lesson."

"Me? Give a lesson? Who to?"

"To a bunch of young wizards and witches who are all starting out on their own magical journey. With your help, they'll soon achieve level one, hopefully."

"You mean, like, be a teacher?"

"Only if you can learn to speak properly first. '*You mean, like, be a teacher?*' Was that supposed to be a sentence?"

"Sorry. You just caught me off-guard. Do you mean you want me to teach them?"

"That's precisely what I mean. Witchcraft is all about paying it forward."

"But, I'm busy! I've got cases to work on."

"Jill, you and I both know that any time you spend in

Candlefield does not impact on your time here in the human world. So, giving a lesson to a few children is not going to have any effect on this silly little business of yours."

"Excuse me! This is not a 'silly little business'. And, even though time stands still, it still uses up my energy."

"Aww, you poor thing."

I might have known better than to expect any sympathy. "So where am I supposed to give this lesson?"

"In the Range, of course. Come on, they've been waiting for five minutes already."

"Why didn't you tell me about this before now? I haven't had chance to prepare."

"Be quiet with your excuses." She held out her bony hand.

It was pointless arguing once Grandma had made up her mind, so I took her hand, and the next thing I knew, we were standing in the Range. It was quite a while since I'd been there. My mind went back to my very first visit with Grandma and the twins. At the time, I'd been on level one. When Grandma had asked me to perform the 'transform' spell, I'd had no idea that it was a level five spell. It was after that I began to realise I had the potential to become a great witch.

"Earth to Jill. Are you with us?" Grandma's voice brought me back down to earth with a thud.

"Yeah, sorry — I was just — err — yeah I'm back."

"Good. It's time for you to meet your pupils." She led the way to a quiet section of the Range where a bunch of young witches and wizards were waiting. There were eight of them in total: Four boys and four girls. They all looked at me expectantly.

"Right, boys and girls," Grandma said. "As promised, your teacher will be Jill Gooder. I assume you've all heard of her?" They all nodded. "Good. In that case, I'll leave you in Miss Gooder's capable hands."

She leaned forward and whispered, "Don't mess this up."

Before I could respond, she'd disappeared.

"Hello, everyone."

"Hello, Miss Gooder!" They all said in unison.

"I think you should call me Jill."

"We can't do that," a young witch at the front said. "We're not allowed to call teachers by their first name."

"Who says?"

"We were all given a book of rules. One of them is that you must always address teachers by their surname."

"Okay, Miss Gooder it is then. That lady was my grandma, but I suppose you already know that?"

They all nodded.

"You all said you've heard of me? How?"

All hands went up; I pointed to one of the young wizards at the front.

"What's your name?"

"Donald, Miss."

"Hello, Donald. How have you heard of me?"

"You're the witch who got into the sealed room at the Museum of Witchcraft."

"That's right, Donald. I did."

"My mum says, you must be the most powerful witch there's ever been because no one else has ever been able to get into that room. Is that right, Miss?"

"I'm not sure about that, Donald. I'm actually still only a level three witch."

Another hand shot up; a young witch, this time.

"What's your name?"

"Lydia, Miss Gooder. My dad says you should be a level six witch for getting into the sealed room, and for all the competitions you've won."

"That's very nice of your dad, but I have to work my way through the levels unless I win the Levels Competition next year."

"You will win it, Miss! My dad says you definitely will!"

"We'll have to see. Anyway, I suppose we ought to get started with the lesson. Look, I'm going to be honest with you. I'm not really a teacher. I didn't even know I was going to be taking this class until about five minutes ago, so I haven't prepared anything. Maybe, we could focus on one spell, and see how it goes? How do you feel about that?"

They all nodded enthusiastically.

Being there with them made me realise what I'd missed out on as a kid. Their enthusiasm for learning magic was clear to see. They would have many years to develop their skills whereas I'd been totally unaware that I was a witch, so had grown up without magic in my life.

"Why don't we start with something fairly simple: The 'faster' spell. Do you all know that one?" They all nodded. "Are you sure?"

One hand went up. A young wizard.

"Yes, what's your name?"

"Tim, Miss Gooder. I don't know it. I'm sorry."

"That's okay, Tim. That's what you're here to learn. Do you all have your Book of Spells with you?"

They grabbed their bags, and pulled out a copy of the same book that I'd once been given by Aunt Lucy.

"I tell you what. Why don't you all spend a few minutes looking at the 'faster' spell. Then we'll give it a try, and see how you get on. Don't worry if you find it difficult to remember the images at first. I was hopeless when I started."

That seemed to make them relax a little.

"I'll take a walk around the Range while you study the spell."

I figured if I walked around the perimeter, it would give them plenty of time to swot up on the spell. I passed by several groups of witches and wizards—all at different stages of the learning process. I spotted at least a dozen level six witches. Whereas at one time, they wouldn't have even noticed me, today they all seemed to be watching me. It made me a little self-conscious.

"What gives you the right to teach a class?" The familiar, but unwelcome voice came from behind me. I turned around to find my BFF, Alicia.

"Grandma asked me to take it, if you must know."

"You've no right to be teaching witches and wizards. You're not even a proper witch yourself."

"Nice to see you too. How's Ma Chivers?"

"If I had my way, you wouldn't be allowed to take these lessons. I've already spoken to Ma Chivers about it. She's not very happy. She says she's going to bring it up with the other level six witches."

"That's fine by me. I'll be happy to stand down if that's what people want. But for now, I've been asked to take this class, and that's what I'm going to do. So, if you don't mind, Alicia, there are some young witches and wizards waiting for me."

She huffed and puffed, but didn't make any attempt to stop me.

When I got back to the kids, they were still poring over the page for the 'faster' spell.

"Right, everyone. Time to put your books away." I waited until they had. "On the count of three, I want you to cast the spell, and then run to that wall on the far side of the Range. Then turn around and run back. Okay? One, two, three."

The concentration was etched on their faces. One by one, they all set off, running at breakneck speed towards the wall.

All except one, that is.

Tim was still standing there with his eyes closed.

"Tim? Are you okay?"

"I keep getting the images mixed up, Miss. I'm sorry."

"Don't worry about it. I think you're trying a little too hard. Take your book back out again."

"But Miss, I'm meant to have memorised it."

"It doesn't matter about that. It's more important that you prove to yourself you can cast the spell." I flicked through the book until I reached the 'faster' spell. "There you are. Look at the images, cast the spell, and then off you go."

The spell worked perfectly. He ran to the wall and back again, finishing only a few yards behind the others.

"That's very good, everyone. I don't know how often we'll be having these lessons, but there's something very important I want to tell you. You mustn't spend every spare minute on this. It's important you find time to be with your friends, and for play. You should try to devote no more than one hour each day to studying this book. When we have our next lesson, I'll pick one spell, and we'll make sure that you're able to master it. Before we finish today, does anyone have any questions?"

All their hands went up.

"Lydia?"

"Will you sign my spell book, please, Miss Gooder?"

"Sign your book?"

"Please, Miss."

"And mine!"

"And mine!"

Wow! Kathy, eat your heart out.

*** 

I was making remarkably little progress in the Starr Fish murder case. Even so, I thought I'd better give Stuart Steele an update. I preferred to do it at a time that suited me rather than have him contact me out of the blue. If he was to call when Jack was with me, it could have been very embarrassing.

So, after I'd finished signing autographs for my young fans —

What? If Kathy can have fans, then I'm sure a superstar witch like me can.

Anyway, as I was saying. I magicked myself over to Bar Fish, in the hope that he'd be there.

I was out of luck. The bar manager told me that Stuart was out of town for a couple of days. I asked him what he made of his boss.

"I knew Stuart long before he opened Bar Fish. He used

to come into the bar where I worked previously, on the other side of Washbridge. That's how I landed this job. He liked the way I ran the bar, and asked if I'd do the same for him here. It sounded like a great opportunity. It was a lot more money."

"I'm sensing there's a 'but' coming?"

"There have been a lot of rumours recently."

"What kind of rumours?"

"I shouldn't really say."

"Come on. I won't tell anyone."

"Rumours that Stuart overspent putting this place together, and that the money's run out. I overheard him on the phone to his accountant—or maybe the bank. He said something about cash-flow problems. And he hasn't been himself recently. He always used to be a happy-go-lucky guy. Maybe it's just the pressure he's been under, but he's been really short with everyone. I'm worried about whether or not the bar is going to survive, and if I'll still have a job. I don't think it helped that Stuart's girlfriend dumped him."

"Do you know why?"

"No idea. He wouldn't talk about it."

"I don't suppose you know how I can get in touch with her, do you?"

"I do, actually. Stuart gave me her phone number in case I couldn't reach him any time."

# Chapter 20

I was in the outer office with Mrs V when the door burst open, and Armi came rushing in. He was red-faced and out of breath.

"Armi, are you all right?" Mrs V looked concerned, and little wonder.

"I'm fine." He gasped. "Just let me catch my breath."

"Would you like a glass of water?" I offered.

"No, it's okay. I'm all right. I'm glad I caught you both together, though."

"Whatever's wrong?" Mrs V said.

"It's Gordon."

"I might have guessed." My blood pressure could rise just at the mention of his name. "What's he done now?"

"He thinks he's found a way to have you thrown out."

"He's tried before and failed. What's he up to this time?"

"He's got a picture of a cat sitting in your windowsill."

Oh, bum.

Mrs V gave me a look; she knew that we weren't meant to have Winky in the office.

"I don't see how he can, Armi. We don't have any cats in here," I lied.

"Look, Jill, you don't have to lie to me. I've seen the cat myself, but I don't care. I love animals, and cats in particular. But I do know that it's against the terms of the lease. When Gordon tells Zac, things might get very difficult for you. There's something else, and I know this is going to sound crazy."

"Go on."

"I've seen the photo, and it looks like the cat is—" He

hesitated. "No, it's too ridiculous."

"Go on, Armi, spit it out."

"It actually looks like the cat is waving flags around."

Mrs V looked puzzled. Me, not so much.

"Flags?" I tried to sound shocked.

"I told you that you'd think I was crazy."

"I'm pretty sure a cat can't wave flags, Armi," Mrs V said.

Little did she know.

"Anyway, I've got to get back. I wanted to warn you both because I'm sure Gordon has called the landlord already. When he gets here, and Gordon shows him the photograph, things might be very difficult for you."

"Okay. Thanks for the heads-up." I forced a smile.

"See you later, Armi." Mrs V blew him a kiss.

"How sweet." I grinned.

"Never mind that, Jill. What are we going to do about Gordon Armitage? I warned you that stupid cat would get us into trouble."

"Don't worry about it. I'll sort something out."

"But if he has a photo, we'll be thrown out for sure."

"Mrs V, I've already told you. Don't worry. I've got this one."

I knew that Gordon Armitage regularly popped out to his favourite coffee shop. He was a creature of habit, and made the trip at more or less the same time, once in the morning, and again in the afternoon. He could have sent a junior, but I suspected he was also going out for a crafty cigarette. A few minutes before his morning run, I waited behind the vending machine in the common area. When Gordon appeared, I stepped out in front of him.

"Gooder! You made me jump! What are you trying to do now? Give me a heart attack?"

Don't give me ideas.

"Sorry, Gordon. I was just picking up the coin I dropped. I didn't see you there."

"A likely story. Get out of my way."

"Time for a cigarette break, Gordon?"

"I don't smoke. Now move!"

Before he could side-step me, I cast the 'sleep' spell, and managed to catch him as he slumped to the floor. His phone was in the outer pocket of his jacket. Fortunately, he hadn't set a password, so I flicked through the screens, and brought up his gallery of photographs. Sure enough, the most recent one on there was of Winky, and he was indeed waving his little flags around. If Zac saw this, he'd have no option but to throw me out. I had to do something, and I had to do it quickly.

First things first. I dragged Gordon into the cleaners' cupboard—I couldn't have people tripping over him. Next, I popped back into my office.

"Mrs V, get your knitting needles, and go stand by the window in my office. The one where Winky usually sits."

"Why?"

"Please, just do it. There's no time to explain."

"What do you want me to do there?"

"Wave your knitting needles around as though you're signalling to someone."

"People will think I'm crazy."

"You have to trust me."

She sighed. "I hope you know what you're doing."

So did I.

I didn't have very long because Zac would arrive at any moment, so I rushed downstairs, out of the building, and waited until Mrs V appeared at my window. She looked rather self-conscious, but began to wave the knitting needles around, as instructed.

I took a photo on Gordon's phone, and then deleted the one of Winky. After rushing back inside, I put the phone back in Gordon's pocket, pulled him out of the cupboard, and reversed the spell.

"What happened? What am I doing on the floor?"

"You tripped. Are you all right?"

"Something weird is going on here."

"You're just clumsy, that's all."

"I'm not the least bit clumsy. Not normally. That's the effect you have on me." He climbed back to his feet. "Get out of my way."

A few minutes later, Mrs V came into my office. "The landlord is here."

I followed her into the outer office. "Hello, Zac."

"Hi, Jill. Needless to say I'm here because of Gordon again. He insists that you're keeping a cat in the office. He reckons he has a photo of it." He sighed. "Waving flags."

"A cat waving flags?"

"That's what he says."

"Do you think maybe he has a drink problem?"

Just then, Gordon came charging into the office.

"I heard that. No, I don't have a drink problem, but what I do have is photographic evidence. What can't speak, can't lie." He took out his phone. "Look, Zac, see?" He brought up the most recent photograph.

"Gordon," Zac said. "Is this meant to be the

photograph?"

"Yes! That's the one." Gordon didn't even bother to look at the screen. He was too busy gloating.

"But that's a photograph of Jill's receptionist. And, from what I can see, she's holding knitting needles in her hands. There's no sign of any flags. Or cats."

"That's not the photograph," Gordon insisted. "The photograph I had was of a cat waving flags."

"Where is it, then?"

"I don't know. It's disappeared." He turned to me. "You've done it again, Gooder. You've sabotaged me! It was a cat! I saw it with my own eyes! I'm not crazy!"

"Hmm? The jury's still out on that one." I grinned.

"I — err — you — err — I'll get you, Gooder." With that, he stormed out of my office.

"Once again, Jill." Zac looked and sounded exasperated. "I can only apologise."

***

After some persuasion, I'd managed to get Stuart Steele's ex-girlfriend to agree to talk to me. Her name was Brie Lant. She answered the door dressed as though she was just on her way to a wedding or a posh restaurant, but I had a suspicion that she always dressed to impress. Her makeup was immaculate. She obviously spent a fortune at the hairdresser. Everything about her screamed money, and yet the apartment she lived in was quite a modest one, which didn't seem to fit in with the rest of her image.

"Hi, I'm Jill Gooder, I called earlier?"

"Oh yah. Do come in."

*Oh yah?* Oh boy!

"You do realise I'm no longer seeing Stuart?"

"Yes, so I understand, but I still think you may be able to help. I'm investigating the murder of Starr Fish. You've probably heard about it in the news."

"Wasn't she in one of those ghastly reality TV shows?"

"Yes. She was found dead in Bar Fish, which as you probably know is Stuart's Steele's new venture."

"And what an unmitigated disaster that's been." She moved towards the glass-fronted cabinet. "I'm having a glass of wine. Would you care for one?"

"Not for me thanks."

She poured herself a large glass of rose, and took much more than a sip.

"How do you mean, disaster?"

"I tried to warn him, but he wouldn't listen. Who wants to sit in a bar surrounded by fish? The riff raff, that's all. And *those* kind of people don't have money to spend. Not *real* money."

"*Those* kind of people?"

"You know the kind. Dirty finger nails and no dress sense."

"You weren't keen on the idea, then?"

"There are far better ways to spend money. He'd promised to move me into a new apartment, and to buy me a new car, but once he started on that crazy venture, that all went out of the window."

"Had you and he been seeing each other for long?"

"Oh, yah — ages. At least two months."

"What attracted you to him?"

"He was very generous. At first."

"And good looking?"

"I suppose so."

I was beginning to wonder if she'd even be able to pick him out in a line-up. Probably, provided he had his wallet in his hand.

"Why did you split up?"

"Because of the stupid Bar Fish venture, why do you think? We'd probably still be together if it wasn't for that."

"So, you're saying you split up because of the money he was ploughing into Bar Fish?"

"He'd promised me an apartment, and a car."

"Of course."

"I told him, it was either Bar Fish or me."

"I'm guessing he chose Bar Fish."

"Yah, and he's welcome to it."

Brie Lant was a nasty piece of work; an unapologetic gold digger, but she had at least provided me with some useful information. According to Brie, Stuart had got in way too deep — that seemed to correspond with what the bar manager had told me, and might explain Stuart's personality change.

Maybe I'd been looking at this case from the wrong angle altogether?

I had a hunch.

"Hello. Is that BeeLine motors?"

"That's us, what can I do you for?"

"My name is Brie Lant. You collected my boyfriend's car for repair the other day."

"I doubt that."

"I haven't even told you his name yet."

"You don't need to. We don't repair cars. We repossess

them."

"Repossess?"

"As in when someone doesn't keep up their payments."

"I think there must be a mistake."

"There always is."

"What if I was to pay the money owed?"

"You have ten days from the day the car is repossessed. Plus, there's our charges on top to pay."

"Sure. Can you tell me how much that will be?" I gave him Stuart's name and address.

"Three thousand, two hundred and eighty-five pounds."

"Is a credit card okay?"

"Sure."

"Will it be possible to see the car first. Just to make sure it's not damaged in any way?"

"Sure."

"Can I look inside it?"

"Yes, someone will show you, but we can't let you have the keys."

"Why not?"

"Because we don't want people driving off before they've paid."

"Of course. Okay, I'll come right over."


BeeLine Motors was essentially a massive car pound. There were cars of every type, size and colour as far as the eye could see. At the front of the pound was a small office where I had to wait in line. The man behind the counter looked terminally bored when I passed him Stuart Steele's details.

"I'm his girlfriend."

"You could be his long lost cousin for all I care. Provided you've got the money."

"When I called earlier, you said I could see the car before I made the payment."

"Ten minutes only."

He pressed a buzzer, and moments later, a young man with a nose piercing, appeared from the back.

"Chops, take this lady down to G327."

I followed the young man, down the lines of cars.

"Chops? Is that really your name?"

"Nah. It's just what Bill calls me. He thinks it's funny."

"What *is* your name?"

"David."

"David? I don't get it."

"David Lamb."

"Lamb?" I laughed. "Lamb chops?"

He shot me a look.

"Sorry. Not funny."

"Is this your car, love?"

"No, it's my boyfriend's."

"You only get ten minutes."

"That's fine."

In fact, it took me less than a minute. As soon as I checked the boot, I had my answer.

"You have to go back to the office to pay," Chops said.

"Nah. I don't think I'll bother. You can keep it."

# Chapter 21

According to the bar manager at Bar Fish, Stuart Steele was due home late that evening, so I made sure I was at his house before he arrived. It was easy to gain access with a combination of the 'power' and 'take it back' spells. He would have no idea I'd forced the lock.

The house was rather creepy. It felt like there were hundreds of eyes on me—which of course there were. Tropical fish of all shapes, sizes and colours stared out from the tanks on the walls, and under the floor. I headed for the living room where I took a sample of the water from the large open-topped tank.

Now, all I had to do was wait.

It was almost a quarter-past-ten when a taxi pulled up outside. Stuart paid the driver, and moments later, walked into the living room. When he spotted me, he dropped his briefcase.

"Jill? What are you doing here? How did you get in?"

"Never mind that, I have a question for you."

"What?"

"Why did you kill Starr Fish?"

"Me?" He laughed or at least tried to. It was hardly convincing. "Kill her? Don't be ridiculous. I was the one who asked you to find out who murdered her."

"And that's precisely what I've done, but we both know the real reason you hired me, don't we? You thought you'd be able to find out how the police investigation was going through my connection with Jack."

"This is crazy. Why would I kill her? I didn't even know the woman."

"Really? Didn't you book her to do a personal appearance at Bar Fish?"

"No. That's rubbish."

"I don't think so. Starr was handling her own bookings, and kept surprisingly good records." I lied.

"Okay. I did book her, but like I said, it didn't work out."

"It didn't work out because you couldn't pay her. She was your last hope, wasn't she?"

"What are you talking about?"

"The money had run out, and the bank was threatening to foreclose. You needed a miracle. You thought having Starr Fish in your bar would generate enough publicity to give the business a boost to get you through. She was the biggest thing that's happened in Washbridge forever. My guess is that when your cheque bounced, she came around here to confront you."

"She's never been here."

"Why did you kill her, Stuart? Did she laugh in your face when you tried to persuade her to wait for her money? Did she tell you to shove your tropical fish where the sun doesn't shine?"

"This is all nonsense."

"Your last hope had gone, and you saw red. You probably didn't intend to kill her. But then you realised that, even dead, she could still provide the publicity you needed. So you took her body to Bar Fish, put her in the tank and tipped off Pullman. You knew he'd bite because he'd taken pictures of Starr Fish before."

"I've told you, she was never here. She drowned at Bar Fish. I had nothing to do with it."

"You're lying. She wasn't drowned at Bar Fish. The

water in her lungs doesn't match the water in the tanks there, but I'm guessing it will match the water in the tanks here." I held up the test tube, which contained the sample I'd taken earlier. "Would you like a small wager? And there are traces of Starr in your repossessed car. The boot is still damp."

He slumped into the chair, and I knew I'd got him.

"I didn't mean to drown her. She just wouldn't listen to reason. She'd waited until the last minute to pull out; there wasn't time to get anyone else. I told her I'd make sure she was paid, but she wanted the money upfront. I didn't have it. She told me to stuff it, and I lost it. It's all a blur. I thought if I scared her, she'd agree to do it, but then she stopped breathing."

"And, instead of doing the decent thing—calling the police—you were still only thinking about yourself. Starr Fish could be even bigger news now she'd been murdered."

"I needed the publicity. I was going to lose everything!"

"You're going to get plenty of publicity now, Stuart, but I'm not sure it's going to do you or Bar Fish any good."

I called Jack.

***

An hour later, Stuart Steele had been taken away— under arrest for the murder of Starr Fish. Jack was giving me a lift back to my car which I'd parked a few streets away.

"I suppose I'd be wasting my breath telling you that you shouldn't have confronted him alone?" Jack was decidedly unhappy.

"I was never in any danger."

"He'd already murdered one woman in that house."

"I can handle myself, Jack. You know that."

He went silent on me, but I decided it was probably best to leave it rather than cause a big row. When he pulled up behind my car, I reached for the door handle.

"Jill wait! We need to talk."

Oh bum.

Call me pessimistic, but that sounded ominous. Was he planning to dump me? I couldn't blame him if he did. Our relationship had been cursed right from the start. Perhaps it really *was* cursed. Maybe Grandma had cast a spell on us; I wouldn't put it past her. Perhaps she didn't like the idea of me going out with a human.

"I'm sorry I didn't call you before I confronted him," I said.

"This isn't about that."

"What then?"

"There's something else we need to talk about."

Oh dear. Here comes the *'it's not you, it's me'* speech.

"Look, it's probably best if I get straight to the point."

Here it comes. I knew it.

"I've been trying to figure out what's been going wrong between us."

Let me guess. It's you, not me.

"It's not us. It's our circumstances."

Was that a variation on the *'it's not you, it's me'* speech? I waited for him to continue.

"I'm not expressing myself very well. What I'm trying to say is I think a lot of the problem stems from the fact that we barely see one another."

"That's true."

"Anyway, I guess what I'm getting at is—err—I think our relationship might have a better chance if we spent more time together. If you were to move into my place."

I was stunned. More than stunned. It had never occurred to me for a moment that he was going to suggest that. "You mean live together?"

"Yeah."

"I don't know what to say."

"Does the idea appal you?"

"No, of course not. It's just that I wasn't expecting it."

"What were you expecting?"

"I don't know, but not this. It's a big step."

"I realise that. I'm not suggesting you give up your flat. We could see how things go. If it doesn't work out, you could just move back. But if things do work out, we can take it from there. What do you say?"

"I'm going to need some time to think about it. Is that okay?"

"Of course. Take as long as you like, but I'm worried if we carry on as we are at present that we may end up breaking up altogether."

"I know. You're right. I'll let you have my decision as soon as I can."

"Okay. Goodnight, then."

I was still stunned as I watched him drive away. Jack was right—our so-called relationship was headed nowhere fast, but I'd still been blindsided by his suggestion that we live together. Of course, he had no idea what my main reservations were. How could he? The question I had to ask myself was could I live a lie every day?

***

I managed virtually no sleep that night. Did I want to move in with Jack? That was easy—of course I did. But was it fair on him? He'd never be able to know the *real* me. I'd never be able to tell him that I was a witch. It would all have been so much easier if I'd never found out.

I was pretty much useless at work, although I did manage to categorise every paper clip and rubber band in the office. Even Winky asked if I was feeling okay.

I needed to talk to someone, and although I couldn't mention the whole 'witch' thing, I wanted that someone to be Kathy. Growing up, we'd always confided in one another. Despite our differences, I still valued her opinion. I called and arranged to go over after she'd finished at Ever.

"Auntie Jill, Auntie Jill, come and see the beanies." Lizzie collared me as soon as I walked in the door.

"I need to talk to your mummy."

Ever since Kathy and Lizzie had *abducted* my beanies, I dreaded seeing them. The two of them had insisted on cutting several of them in half, and then joining the two halves together to make Frankensteinesque monsters. It tore me apart to see it.

"Please, Auntie Jill. I want you to see this." She grabbed my hand, and led me to her bedroom.

"Why are all the beanies hanging by their necks from the ceiling, Lizzie?"

"Before we did this, I couldn't find the one I wanted because they were all over the floor."

"Maybe if you'd catalogued and categorized them as I

suggested, there wouldn't have been a problem."

"That's boring. This is much better. It was Mummy's idea."

Why didn't that surprise me?

"Mummy said we could have a line across the room, and then hang the beanies from it. It's great, isn't it, Auntie Jill?"

"Do you think the beanies enjoy hanging by their necks?"

"Yes, they love it."

"What happens when you want to play with one of them?"

"If I stand on my footstool, I can take their head out of the loop."

Noose, more like.

"Look, I'll show you." She stepped onto the footstool, reached up, and took my favourite beanie bear out of its noose. The poor thing must have been hanging there for ages. It was a travesty.

"Where's all of your Lego gone?" I'd grown accustomed to having to step over the little bricks whenever I visited Kathy's, but today there were none to be seen.

"I like virtual building now."

"What's that?"

"I'll show you on my tablet."

"You've got a tablet?"

"Yes, Mummy bought one each for Mikey and me. Look!" Her tiny fingers skipped back and forth across the screen. "This is the app." On screen, there were lots of little building blocks, similar to the ones she used to play with in real life. "This is how I build." She put her finger on the virtual blocks, and began to build a wall. Then she picked up a window, and slid it into the wall she'd just created. "See how easy it is, Auntie Jill? Do you want to have a go?"

"No thanks. I'm not very good with tablets."

"That's what Mummy said."

"Did she now? Where is your mummy anyway?"

"I think she's in the kitchen."

"I need to have a word with her. Why don't you build me something on your tablet, and come and show me when it's finished?"

"Okay. I'll build you a princess's palace."

"That would be nice." If rather stereotypical.

"Kathy, why are you teaching your daughter to hang things?"

"You've seen the beanies, then?"

"Yes, I've seen them. The poor things are hanging from nooses."

"They're only soft toys, Jill. They don't have feelings."

"You see, that's where you're wrong. Soft toys *do* have feelings."

"You're crazy. Anyway, what brings you around here? If you're here for dinner again, I'm going to have to start charging you."

"Relax. That's not why I came over. I need your advice."

"Is that a joke? When did you ever listen to *my* advice?"

"That just goes to show how desperate I am."

"Thanks, Jill."

"Jack has asked me to move in with him."

Kathy sat down. "Wow! Wow! Wow!"

"Is that all you can say?"

"I didn't see that one coming."

"Neither did I. I thought he was going to dump me, but then he suggested I move in with him."

"What did you say?"

"Not a lot, really. I was too surprised. Just that I needed time to think about it."

"I bet he was thrilled by your enthusiasm."

"What was I meant to do? I couldn't just say 'yes' without at least thinking about it."

"What would you do with your flat?"

"He suggested I keep it on for a while. Until we've had a chance to see how we get on together."

"Why do you need my advice?"

"Because you're the sensible one in this family."

"By *sensible*, do you mean *boring*?"

"Come on, Kathy. What do you think?"

"I say go for it. What have you got to lose? You've been by yourself for way too long. You have to be prepared to take risks sooner or later. If you end up hating one another, you can always move back to your place. You'd be no worse off than you are now."

"I guess you're right. It's such a big step, though."

"What's the worst that can happen? You get hurt? So what? That's the risk you'll have to take sooner or later if you ever want to find true happiness." She smiled. "Listen to me, I sound like I know what I'm talking about."

"Thanks, Kathy."

# Chapter 22

I was trying to distract myself, but it wasn't easy. Today was the date that had been marked on the wall calendar in The Central. It may have meant nothing, but I couldn't take any chances; I had to be doubly alert. I'd decided to stay in the office all day, and then go straight home.

At least, that had been the plan. But then—

"There's a young man in reception," Mrs V said. "His name is Raven, I think."

"Okay, send him in please, Mrs V."

As soon as he walked through the door, I knew something was wrong.

"What is it?"

"Drake's been kidnapped. Last night, we were together in Washbridge Park when three hooded men appeared from nowhere. One of them hit me over the head. I saw them grab Drake, but I was too stunned to do anything about it."

"Didn't anyone try to help you?"

"It was late; the park was practically empty."

"Do you have any idea who the men were?"

"No, but the chances are TDO is behind it."

"What makes you say that?"

"Because Drake is close to you, and that makes him a target."

Raven was probably right. The thought that this had happened because of me made me feel terrible.

"Why were you in Washbridge, anyway?"

"That's my fault. I've been laying low over here. Drake came to see me. I thought if anyone had a chance of finding him, it would be you. Will you help?"

"What do you want me to do?"

"I'm going back to the park to see if I can find anything, will you put out the feelers in Candlefield?"

"Of course. I'll get straight on it."

We exchanged phone numbers, and promised to make contact if either of us came up with anything.

There were plenty of places one might look for TDO in Candlefield, but today of all days, there was really only one. It was the very last place I wanted to visit, but what choice did I have? Even though my relationship with Drake had never got off the ground, I still considered him a friend.

"I have to go out, Mrs V."

"Is everything okay? That young man looked very worried about something."

"I hope so. A friend of mine has gone missing."

"Have the police been informed?"

"I don't think they'll be able to help this time."

"Be careful, Jill!"

I'd broken through the 'illusion' spell on my previous visit to The Central, and could still see the trapdoor which would give me access to the building. I used my phone to light my way down the stairs, and across the basement. At the bottom of the steps leading into the main building, I hesitated. What was waiting for me up there?

I edged my way up the steps one by one. Once at the top, I peered out between the metal rails which bordered the stairway. The sight that greeted me made my blood run cold. Seated on one of the old wooden chairs was

Drake. His hands appeared to be bound behind his back, and he was wearing a blindfold. Standing next to him was my father. I'd been right all along. TDO was my own father.

"Let him go," I shouted.

My father didn't respond.

"Let Drake go. This is between you and me."

I'd just started to walk towards them, when suddenly, my father began to run towards me.

"Jill, get out of here! It's a trap. Get out!"

I'd been so focussed on my father that I hadn't noticed Drake stand up and remove the blindfold. From there, everything seemed to happen in slow motion. There was a sound so loud it felt as though it might puncture my ear drums. A bolt of lightning hit my father square in the back, and sent him crashing to the ground. It took me a few seconds to realise what had happened. Drake had fired the thunderbolt at my father who was now lying prone on the floor.

I was still trying to process what I'd just seen when someone pushed me from behind, and sent me stumbling forward.

It was Raven.

"Nice of you to come, Jill," Drake said.

"Drake, what's going on? I thought you'd been kidnapped."

"You fell for that? Really? I'm disappointed in you."

"I don't understand."

But even as I said it, I suddenly understood only too clearly.

"You're The Dark One."

"I do hate that name. I'm not even sure who came up

with it. But yes, I suppose I am."

"I thought we were—"

"What? Friends?"

"Friends, yes."

"Then, you're even stupider than I thought."

"What do you want from me?"

"At last, a sensible question. Your mother frustrated my ambitions. By now I should have been the most powerful sup in all of Candlefield. The indisputable ruler of the supernatural world. But just when I was about to take her power, she escaped, and passed it on to you. So you see, I have to take it from you. It's only fair."

"But I don't understand. You could have killed me a dozen times."

"It's true, I could, but some of the power was lost when it passed from your mother to you. What was left wouldn't have been enough for my purposes. I had to wait until you reached level six."

I laughed. "It looks like you've blown it then because I'm still only level three."

"That's true, but now you've inherited the power from the greatest witch of all time: Magna Mondale. That makes you the most powerful witch in Candlefield. And when your power passes to me, it will make me indestructible."

"That's never going to happen."

"What makes you think you have a choice in the matter? You may be the most powerful witch, but you're still no match for me."

I turned to Raven. "Are you going to let your brother do this?"

He laughed.

"You're so naïve, Jill," Drake said. "Raven isn't my brother. He works for me. I believe you've met some of my other followers too?"

"Do you mean those pathetic hooded creatures?"

"No." He seemed to find that amusing. "They were mere puppets which I sent to test you. Don't you think I could have killed you any number of times if I'd wanted to? The Ipod, the explosion—all of those were designed simply to scare you. To encourage you to move up the levels more quickly. The followers I'm referring to are very real, and they're ready to stand behind me when I take control of Candlefield."

"You really are pure evil."

"Thank you. I'll take that as a compliment. Much as I'd like to stand around and talk to you all day, I have more important things to do. Perhaps we should just get this over with."

Just then, there was a rumbling sound—footsteps. The next thing I knew, Grandma and several other level six witches came rushing up the steps from the basement. Raven turned to face them, but they pushed him aside. When he tried to stand up, Grandma thumped him under the chin, knocking him out cold. She might have bony fingers, but when combined with the 'power' spell, she packed a mean punch.

"I see you've brought your family with you." Drake seemed totally unfazed by the intruders.

"I thought I'd find *you* here," Grandma spat the words at Drake. "I didn't trust you from the first moment I met you."

"Did you know he was TDO, Grandma?"

"Not for sure, but I had my suspicions."

So that was why she'd had the surveillance in his flat. It had never been about keeping tabs on me. She'd been watching Drake all along.

Grandma and the other witches formed a semi-circle around him.

"Give it up, Drake," Grandma said. "You can't get out of here."

He laughed. "Do you really think you're a match for me?"

"We'll find out." Grandma shot a thunderbolt at him; the other witches did the same.

Just as the thunderbolts were about to find their mark, he raised his hand, and the thunderbolts flew back towards Grandma and the others, knocking them flat on their backs. Grandma wasn't dead, but she was stunned — as were the other witches.

"That leaves just you and me, Jill. Shall we get this over with?" Drake began to walk towards me. This was it. I was done for, unless I could somehow overcome him. But what chance did I have if so many level six witches had already failed?

But I wasn't about to give up — I would at least go down fighting.

First, I had to get out of the way. He was approaching quickly, and any moment, he would be on top of me. A combination of the 'power' and 'vortex' spells allowed me to move at lightning speed, and not just in a straight line. I spun round in circles until I was behind Drake. As he turned to see where I'd gone, I took hold of one of the metal rails which bordered the steps to the basement, using the 'power' spell to dislodge it from the floor. Then I combined that same spell with the 'propel' spell to launch the rail like a spear.

Drake laughed, and put up his hand to deflect it—just as he'd done with the thunderbolts that Grandma and the other witches had shot at him. But the spear pierced his hand, and then pierced his forehead.

He looked momentarily stunned, but then fell backwards onto the floor. He was dead. I'd killed Drake. I'd killed TDO.

Grandma had managed to get to her knees.

"Grandma, are you okay?"

"Of course I'm okay. What about you?"

"I'm fine."

The other witches appeared to be all right too, and were slowly getting back to their feet. But what about my father? He'd tried to save me from Drake who must have forced him to stand next to the chair in the hope that I'd kill my own father.

I ran over to him.

"Dad? Dad?"

I felt for his pulse, but there was nothing. The power of Drake's thunderbolt must have killed him instantly.

I'd always assumed my father didn't love me—that he didn't care. I'd been so very wrong. His very last act had been to try to save me. When last I'd seen him, I'd told him I wanted nothing more to do with him, and had said 'goodbye'. What wouldn't I have given to speak to him one more time? To tell him that I loved him. But it was too late. He had gone.

# Chapter 23

Grandma came rushing into my office.

"Come on Jill, we have to get going. There's no time to lose."

"No time to lose for *what*? Please tell me you haven't arranged another lesson already. I've got work to do."

"It has nothing to do with lessons; there's an EGM for the level six witches."

"No chance! I don't ever want to go to another EGM. Last time, they pulled me onto the stage, and interrogated me about Magna's book. I'm staying well clear. Take Aunt Lucy with you if you need an assistant."

"The only reason the EGM has been called is because of you. You have to be there."

"Because of me? Do they want to interrogate me again? Can't you tell them I threw the book into the Dark Well?"

"It has nothing to do with Magna's book. There's nothing for you to worry about this time, I promise. But we have to go, and we have to go right now."

It was pointless arguing, so I took hold of Grandma's hand, and she magicked us to the town hall in Candlefield.

There were numerous level six witches on their way inside. When they saw me they all smiled. What a very different reception to the one I'd received at the previous EGM. Back then, I'd been given the cold shoulder by all and sundry. Today, they were not only smiling at me, but a few of them actually waved and called out my name.

Grandma hurried me into the hall. I pointed to two empty seats at the back of the room.

"You need to be right at the front, young lady."

"What? No, please!"

"Come on." She took hold of my arm, and practically frogmarched me to the front of the hall where she insisted we sit at a table in the front row. All the witches around us were smiling and waving at me. It was all a little unnerving if I'm honest. At least on the previous occasion, I'd known where I stood. This time, I didn't know what to expect. Five minutes later, the doors were closed; the room was full to capacity.

A witch took to the stage. It was the same woman who had interrogated me the last time I was there. Today though, she looked much happier; she too smiled at me. This was really starting to creep me out.

"Level six witches, welcome to this Extraordinary General Meeting. Most of you will already know why we're here."

Really? I didn't have a clue.

"For too many years, Candlefield has lived under a shadow. That shadow was cast by an evil sup known as The Dark One. For the longest time, we level six witches have sought to put a stop to his reign of terror, but failed even to identify him. But today, I am pleased to report that The Dark One is no more."

The room was filled with cheers and applause, which went on for several minutes.

"You may recall that Jill Gooder was brought before the last EGM to answer questions about Magna Mondale's book. At that time, I think most of us were concerned that she was too inexperienced to be in possession of such a powerful tool. We were wrong. TDO tried to kill Jill, so that he could acquire her powers. Had he succeeded, no one would have been able to stand in his way. Several level six witches, including Jill's own grandmother confronted TDO in an attempt to save Jill, but he was too powerful for them. That seemed to leave Jill at his mercy, and with it the future of Candlefield. But, as you can see, Jill is with us here today. She single-handedly rid us of TDO once and for all."

At that, the hall once again erupted in cheers. It seemed as though everyone was on their feet, even Grandma.

"Jill, please will you join me on stage."

I hesitated—I was more than a little embarrassed by all the attention, but Grandma ushered me onto the stage.

"Would you say a few words, please, Jill?"

Oh dear, I hated speaking in public.

I tapped the microphone. "Can everyone hear me? Good. Thank you for those kind words. I'm obviously thrilled that TDO is no more, but I'm equally saddened that my father was killed trying to save me. I barely knew my father, and I'm ashamed to say I thought he didn't care about me, and even that he might actually be TDO. I know now I was wrong, but it's too late to tell him. So, as I'm sure you will understand, it is with mixed feelings that I accept your thanks."

I started to walk off the stage, but the woman grabbed my arm.

"Just a moment, Jill. I'd like you to stay there for a little longer."

Before I could object, she'd turned to address the room again.

"Level six witches, there is only one motion in front of us today. That motion is to create a new level of witchcraft—level seven. The reason for doing that should be obvious to everyone. It is to recognise that we now have among us a witch who is far more powerful than any level six witch has ever been. In the same way that level six was created for Magna Mondale, we should now create another level for Jill Gooder."

"No, hold on!" I stepped forward.

"Jill, please." She put her hand out to silence me. "Can we have a show of hands. All those in favour of creating level seven, please raise your hand."

This was the same motion that had been defeated at the last AGM – a motion that Grandma had pushed hard for. This time though, it seemed that every hand in the room was raised.

"Thank you, ladies. All those against?"

There was only one hand raised. Ma Chivers glared at me, defiantly.

"The motion is passed, almost unanimously. Jill, I would like to invite you to become the first level seven witch."

\*\*\*

After the EGM had finished, I left Grandma inside talking to some of her friends. Outside on the steps, someone called my name. It was Ma Chivers.

"I suppose you think you've won." As always she was right in my face.

"I wasn't aware it was a competition. You'll be sorry to have lost your leader."

"What leader?"

"TDO of course."

She laughed. "TDO was never my 'leader'. He was only ever the pretender to the throne."

"What are you talking about?"

"You'll find out soon enough." She laughed again. "The Phoenix will make sure of that."

"Who?"

She walked away without another word. Why was I even wasting my time with her? She had always been full of it.

*\*\**

I magicked myself to Washbridge, and was on my way back to the office when someone called my name.

"Jill, we were just on our way to see you." It was Bonnie and Clive. "We have that present we promised you." Clive passed me a rectangular package wrapped in pretty floral gift-wrap.

"You really shouldn't have."

"Nonsense. It's the least we could do. If it hadn't been for you, and the posters you made, we might never have got our darling Bella back."

That probably wasn't true, but hey, after the day I'd had, I could eat a few chocolates. I could tell from the shape of the present that's what it was.

"Didn't you say you have a cat too?" Clive asked.

"Yes, Winky."

"That's an unusual name."

"He only has one eye."

"Oh dear." Bonnie looked genuinely concerned. "Poor little man. How does he cope?"

"He seems to get by."

"We'd better not keep you. I'm sure you're busy."

"As always."

I couldn't wait to get stuck into the chocolates, but maybe I should offer Mrs V one.

What? Okay, maybe two. But I was going to take out my favourites first.

I tore off the gift wrap.

Oh bum! It wasn't chocolates.

"Winky? Where are you?"

"What's up?" He crawled out from under my desk.

"I've got a present for you."

"For me? What's the catch?"

"Why would you say that? Can't I give my favourite cat a present without an ulterior motive?"

"Unlikely, but go on, I'll bite."

"There you are."

"Wow! Thanks, Jill."

"Do you like it? I had it specially commissioned."

"It's brilliant. It captures Bella's je ne sais quoi."

"That's what I thought."

"It must have cost a few bob. Portraits like this can be expensive."

"Nothing is too good for my darling Winky."

"I'll keep it under the sofa, so I have Bella with me at all times."

How sweet!

\*\*\*

The time had come to let Jack have my answer. It had been one of the most difficult decisions of my entire life. Kathy had been unequivocal that I should say 'yes', but although I valued her opinion, she wasn't privy to all the information.

Could a relationship be built upon a lie? That was the conundrum that had haunted me ever since Jack had posed the question. Even if he never discovered my 'secret', might it eat away at me every day? It would have been so much easier if I hadn't known I was a witch. But I did, and I had to face reality. And the reality was, if I said 'yes', I'd have to live a lie, but if I said 'no', it would spell the end of our relationship forever. Jack and I would be finished before we'd even started.

I'd phoned him an hour ago to tell him I'd made my decision. He'd pressed me to tell him there and then, but I'd refused. It was important to me to do this face to face. He'd been on his way into a meeting, and wasn't sure what time he'd get out. I told him I'd be in Bar Fish, and would wait for him. However long it took.

"What's going to happen to this place?" I asked the bar manager.

He shrugged. "The business is in administration. They're hoping to find a buyer, but I'm not optimistic. I'm already looking for a new job."

"I'm sorry to hear that."

"Fishtail?"

"No, thanks. I need to keep a clear head. I'll have a lime and soda, please."

Every minute seemed a little longer than the previous one. The fish seemed to be taunting me with their wide eyes. I was on my third lime and soda when Jack finally appeared. He looked flustered, and very serious.

"Do you want a drink?" I asked.

"No, I don't want a drink. I have absolutely no idea what the meeting I've just been in was about. I just wanted it to end." He took a seat next to me. "So? What's your answer?"

"I've given this a lot of thought—"

"Enough, Jill. Just tell me what you've decided. Will you move in with me?"

"Yes."

"Yes?" He looked stunned.

"But."

"No 'buts'. Just stick at 'yes'."

"It's only a small 'but'."

"How small?"

"I want to wait for a little while."

"What? Why?"

"Not for long. Just a few months so I can get used to the idea, and to be certain we're both sure about this."

"I'm sure right now. Look at me. Don't I look sure?"

"Yes, but—"

"But you're not sure?"

"No, that's not what I'm saying. I want to do it."

"It doesn't sound like it."

"I do. I absolutely do. More than anything."

"This isn't just your way of letting me down gently?"

"No. I promise."

"How many months?"

"I don't know. Not many."

"One?"

"I don't know."

"Two?"

"Jack!"

"What?"

"Shut up, and kiss me!"

## 12 months later...

Has Jill moved in with Jack? If so, how's that working out?

How is she coping with the responsibility that comes with her new powers?

Is Winky as crazy as ever? (we already know the answer to that one.)

Catch up with Jill Gooder and all your favourite characters (and lots of new ones)

as the adventure continues in the next book:

### Witch Is Why Time Stood Still

(Witch P.I. Mysteries #13)

**More mysteries and even more crazy await you!**

# ALSO BY ADELE ABBOTT

## The Witch P.I. Mysteries:

## The Susan Hall Mysteries:
Whoops! Our New Flatmate Is A Human.
Whoops! All The Money Went Missing.
Whoops! There's A Canary In My Coffee
*See web site for availability.*


**AUTHOR'S WEB SITE**
http:www.AdeleAbbott.com

**FACEBOOK**
http://www.facebook.com/AdeleAbbottAuthor

**MAILING LIST**
(new release notifications only)
http:/AdeleAbbott.com/adele/new-releases/

Made in the USA
San Bernardino, CA
06 October 2018